"Look, Lila, if  for Jessica—" Bru

"But I'm not,"

"Then what d gleam came into think I have an idea why you're here."

Lila lowered her thick eyelashes and smiled coyly. "I think you and I share something, Bruce. A pure and simple desire for revenge."

"What did you have in mind?" Bruce asked, folding his arms across his chest.

"Jessica took something that rightfully belongs to me. The guest spot on Eric Parker's TV program. I want it back, and I plan to get it."

A malicious smile creased Bruce's tanned face. "Ruining Jessica's chance to be on TV also occurred to me as a suitable punishment. But how are we going to do it?"

"Well, I've got a plan." Lila bent forward and related the particulars of her plan to Bruce. When she had finished, Bruce's eyes were glinting with excitement.

"It's perfect," he said. "I always knew you had an evil streak, Lila, but this time you've really outdone yourself."

Lila beamed. "Thank you, Bruce. I think we're going to make a great team."

Bantam Books in the Sweet Valley High series
Ask your bookseller for the books you have missed

# SWEET VALLEY HIGH

# STARRING JESSICA!

### Written by
## Kate William

### Created by
## FRANCINE PASCAL

**BANTAM BOOKS**
NEW YORK · TORONTO · LONDON · SYDNEY · AUCKLAND

RL 6, IL age 12 and up

STARRING JESSICA!
*A Bantam Book / January 1991*

*Sweet Valley High is a registered trademark of Francine Pascal*

*Conceived by Francine Pascal*

*Produced by Daniel Weiss Associates, Inc.*
*33 West 17th Street*
*New York, NY 10011*

*Cover art by James Mathewuse*

ISBN 0-553-28796-6

*Published simultaneously in the United States and Canada*

Bantam Books are published by Bantam Books, a division of Bantam Doubleday Dell
Publishing Group, Inc. Its trademark, consisting of the words "Bantam Books" and
the portrayal of a rooster, is Registered in U.S. Patent and Trademark Office and in
other countries. Marca Registrada. Bantam Books, 666 Fifth Avenue, New York,
New York 10103.

PRINTED IN THE UNITED STATES OF AMERICA

OPM   10   9   8   7   6   5   4   3

*Dedicated to Rod Ritchie and Ben Baglio*

# One

"Applications for everyone," Winston Egbert announced as he passed out a handful of printed sheets to his friends in the Sweet Valley High cafeteria. "Sign up here to be a TV star!"

Jessica Wakefield grabbed one of the applications eagerly, almost falling off her chair in the process. Lila Fowler had reached for the same sheet, and she scowled as her hand came up empty.

"Now, now. No need to fight, girls." Winston offered Lila another form. "There's enough to go around. And let's see a smile, Miss Fowler. Eric Parker's not going to pick a sourpuss to appear on his TV show."

Lila snatched the application from Winston and flashed him a dazzling smile.

1

Jessica laughed. "That fake smile won't fool anybody, Li."

Lila snickered. "Believe me, I wouldn't waste the real thing on Winston. I'm saving my charm for Eric Parker himself."

"I really don't see what all the fuss is about," Elizabeth Wakefield remarked, glancing idly at one of the applications.

Jessica stared at her twin, her eyes wide with disbelief. "You've got to be kidding!" she exclaimed. "Eric Parker is absolutely the most gorgeous man on TV, and he's coming to Sweet Valley next week! He's going to pick one of *us* to do a special guest spot on his talk show. One of *us* is going to be interviewed live on national TV! It'll be a million times more exciting than when I was on Jeremy Frank's local show. We're talking about the big time, Liz!"

Just then, Jessica caught the mischievous twinkle in her twin's eyes. Elizabeth knew as well as anybody what all the fuss was about. She was just teasing Jessica because she knew she had her heart set on being the Sweet Valley High student selected to appear on TV. The special edition of Eric Parker's weekly talk show was called "Growing Up in America."

"Go ahead, give me a hard time," Jessica said. "You'll change your tune when Eric Parker makes me a major celebrity."

"So I take it you've made up your mind to apply for the guest spot," Todd Wilkins, Elizabeth's boyfriend, remarked wryly.

Jessica nodded vehemently. "Isn't everyone going to try for it?" she asked.

Todd shrugged his broad shoulders. "*I'm* not bothering."

"You wouldn't have a chance anyway," interjected Winston. "Eric Parker's looking for a typical high school student, not a superjock."

"And you don't have to be a straight-A student," added Jessica.

"Nope, just an ordinary, all-American, well-rounded type of kid, like Eric Parker probably was when *he* went to Sweet Valley High," Winston said. "What do you say—do I fit the bill or what?"

Aaron Dallas groaned. "If you're all-American, Egbert, this country's in trouble!"

"Are you going to list 'school clown' on your application?" Todd joked.

Winston grinned. "No, I'll just surprise Eric Parker with my incredible wit when he interviews me on his show."

"Unfortunately he'll never get to hear it, because you're not going to be on his show," Lila promised with a toss of her long, light brown hair. "I am."

Winston raised one eyebrow. "You?"

3

"Yeah, right, Li," Jessica said. "You'll be the average American high school student when the average American high school student drives her own sports car and lives in the biggest mansion in town!"

Jessica knew she had Lila there. Her best friend—and occasional enemy—could not deny that her father had made millions in the computer business. As a result of his success, she was the richest girl in Sweet Valley, California.

"I have a lot of interests and special qualities," snapped Lila. "A lot more than you, Jess."

"We'll see about that," Jessica declared hotly.

"Hey, let's keep the competition friendly, girls. This is supposed to be fun," Winston reminded them. "I think everybody would agree we've had enough controversy at Sweet Valley High lately," he added, his tone suddenly serious.

All of the students at the lunch table understood what Winston meant. Not long ago, the high school had been shocked by a racially motivated disturbance. Charlie Cashman, a notorious bully, had caused trouble for Andy Jenkins, a popular black student. Bad feelings had escalated. Coming to understand how such a thing could happen at Sweet Valley High had

4

not been easy; it had been a painful learning experience for the entire student body.

Now Winston turned to Elizabeth. "You're the one I'm worried about beating me out for the TV spot, Liz."

"Well, put your mind at ease," Elizabeth said. "I'm not applying."

"Why not?" Winston asked.

"I just don't have any desire to be on TV," Elizabeth confessed. "To tell you the truth, I think I'd be more comfortable giving the interview than being the person interviewed!" Elizabeth had conducted her share of interviews as a reporter for the school newspaper, *The Oracle;* her latest had been with Claire Middleton, a new student who had made a name for herself at Sweet Valley High by trying out for the boys' football team—and making it.

"You'll do just fine as part of the audience," Jessica assured Elizabeth. "You can be the head of my cheering section!"

Elizabeth smiled. Appearing on a TV talk show was right up Jessica's alley. She loved being in the limelight.

The Wakefield twins' different reactions to the news that a famous TV personality planned to broadcast a program live from Sweet Valley High was typical. The sixteen-year-old sisters were both five feet six inches tall and slender, with shoulder-length silky blond hair, eyes the blue-green shade of the Pacific Ocean, and clear, suntanned complexions. Still, no one who knew them well ever mixed them up— unless Jessica and Elizabeth *wanted* to be mixed up! Certain clues helped their friends distinguish between the twins. Elizabeth often wore her hair up in a ponytail or pulled back with barrettes; Jessica preferred hers loose. And while Elizabeth's taste in clothes was conservative, Jessica enjoyed turning heads by wearing the latest fashions.

But the real difference between the two was not apparent from just looking at them. Elizabeth, older than Jessica by four minutes, was known as the responsible twin. She was a serious student, and her ambition was to be a professional writer. She never missed a deadline for *The Oracle*. But that didn't mean Elizabeth favored all work and no play. She loved writing, but she also loved having a good time with her boyfriend, Todd, and a few special friends. And she was often called upon to head committees at school.

For Jessica, having a good time always came first, with schoolwork placing a distant second. It was a Wakefield family joke that Jessica had plenty of energy when it came to jumping around at cheerleading practice or to getting into trouble, but never when it came to pushing the vacuum cleaner or washing the dishes. Still, it was almost impossible to stay mad at Jessica; Elizabeth knew that better than anyone. Jessica's irresistible charm had gotten her out of more sticky situations than her twin could count—and when her charm didn't work, she could usually count on Elizabeth to bail her out.

Elizabeth listened as Jessica and Winston debated whether Eric Parker was more likely to pick a boy or a girl for the TV interview.

"Since he's a man, it would be more balanced if he picked a girl," Jessica reasoned. "Besides, I'm more photogenic than any boy."

"Modest to the last," quipped Winston. "But I remember a time when you didn't look so photogenic. When we were shipwrecked on Outermost Island."

Jessica grimaced. She remembered only too well the day that the excursion boat the school had chartered ran into a storm. She and Winston had spent a full day and night together on Outermost Island before they were rescued— definitely the longest twenty-four hours of Jessica's life! And it was true that with seaweed in her hair, she had not been looking her best.

"The point I'm trying to make is that people would rather watch a pretty girl than a guy on

7

TV any day," Jessica continued. "Isn't that true, Amy?"

Amy Sutton was gazing idly around the cafeteria. Jessica tapped her friend on the arm to get her attention. "Hey, Amy. This concerns you, you know. You're applying, aren't you?"

"I don't think so," Amy replied. "Eric Parker isn't that hot, if you ask me."

"Not that hot!" Jessica could not believe her ears. Amy was always making fun of Jessica and Lila for their crush on rock star Jamie Peters, and now she wasn't interested in Eric Parker either. "Amy, you just don't know a gorgeous guy when you see one."

"Yes, I do. How about him?"

Jessica followed Amy's gaze, which had zeroed in on a blond, clean-cut boy sitting a few tables away from them. "Tom McKay, from the tennis team?" Jessica was surprised. "He's not bad, but I wouldn't exactly put him in the same category as Eric Parker."

"That's your opinion."

"Since when is Tom McKay your type?" Jessica asked.

"Since I noticed he's ten times cuter than any other guy at this school," Amy retorted. "And I don't think he and Jean are going to be together much longer. Probably because he's been looking for Miss Right."

Jessica shrugged. Who cared whether or not Tom McKay was looking for Miss Right? What really mattered was that Eric Parker was looking for Miss Right, and her name happened to be Jessica Wakefield!

"Let's get back to Eric Parker," Jessica suggested.

"OK, back to Eric Parker," Amy agreed. "According to my mom, he's just another talk-show host with toothpaste-ad teeth and a mannequin's personality."

Amy's mother, Dyan Sutton, was a sportscaster on WXAB, a local television station. Maybe that was why Amy didn't think Eric Parker's broadcasting a show at Sweet Valley High was such a big deal—Amy lived and breathed TV. In fact, she had been the first to know about Eric's special broadcast. Still, Jessica thought, her friend didn't have to ruin everyone else's excitement.

"I bet your mother hasn't even *met* Eric Parker," Jessica declared. "He's a household name all across the country; he moves in the most exclusive circles. WXAB is just kid's stuff."

Amy laughed. "Whatever you say, Jess. I'm on your side, really. Go for it."

*I will*, thought Jessica. Today was Monday—the applications were due on Friday. And next Wednesday, Eric Parker would announce the winner. She folded the paper, kissed it for luck, and carefully tucked it into her shoulder bag. That piece of paper was going to be her ticket to a career on national television!

Jessica sprinted up the stairs to her bedroom. Cheerleading practice had gone overtime, and she was eager to start working on her application.

Jessica paused at the door of her cluttered bedroom, which was nicknamed "The Hershey Bar" by her family because she had chosen to have the walls painted chocolate brown. She knew her desk was in there—somewhere. Jessica rarely sat at it to do homework. She used it more as a dumping ground, and at the moment it was hidden by a small mountain of clothing and magazines.

But she couldn't just slouch on her bed to fill out the application. She needed to make sure that her handwriting was absolutely perfect. Eric Parker would be reading it with his own eyes!

Jessica took the shortcut to her twin's bedroom, through the connecting bathroom. She did not bother to knock; Elizabeth was used to her barging in unannounced.

Elizabeth was at the table she used as a desk,

her fingers flying across the keys of her typewriter. "What's up, Jess?" she asked, looking at her twin.

"This." Jessica dangled the application form in front of Elizabeth's nose. "I'm going to pull up a chair and fill it out right now."

Jessica sat down next to Elizabeth and helped herself to a pen from Elizabeth's ceramic pencil holder. Name, address, age, classes, and grades at Sweet Valley High. Jessica wrote rapidly; that part was easy. Next came a space— a large space—in which to list extracurricular activities, work experience, and hobbies. *Cocaptain of varsity cheerleading squad, member of Pi Beta Alpha sorority, Big Sister/Little Sister program. Tennis, dancing, the beach, boys.* Jessica paused. It wasn't really much of a list, was it? she thought. There was an awful lot of blank space left.

Jessica flipped the application over and stared at the section headed "Plans for the Future." *Plans for the future?* Jessica was dismayed. She didn't *have* any plans for the future, unless you counted planning to save up enough money to buy that suede miniskirt she had been coveting at Lisette's, her favorite boutique in the Valley Mall.

Jessica quickly turned back to her list of interests. *Tennis, dancing, the beach, boys.* . . . Maybe

11

she should cross that last item off. Jessica frowned. When she looked at herself this way, on paper, she almost seemed—was it possible?—a little bit shallow.

"Liz, what am I going to do?" Jessica wailed, tossing the application aside. "Eric Parker's never going to choose me to be on his TV show! I'm not well-rounded!"

Elizabeth smiled. "Don't be silly, Jess. You stand as good a chance as anyone of being chosen."

"But that's not good enough," Jessica pointed out. "I want to be a shoo-in. I want that TV spot! I need that TV spot! It could be the start of my career!"

"What career?"

"Well, my career of being famous."

"OK, let's see." Elizabeth turned off the electric typewriter, picked up Jessica's application, and scanned it quickly. "Here's something you haven't covered in your list: work experience. You baby-sit, and you've had about a million unusual part-time jobs."

Jessica made a sour face. "You mean like selling Tofu-glo beauty products door to door?" she asked skeptically. "Yeah, I really want to include that disaster on my application! This is serious, Liz."

"Well, what about being a candy-striper at the hospital?" Elizabeth reminded her.

"Oh, that's a good one!" Jessica couldn't believe she had forgotten that. She had become a candy-striper just to meet local celebrity Jeremy Frank, who at the time was hospitalized with a broken leg. Candy-striping had led to her first TV appearance! Back then, Jessica had thought that Jeremy Frank was the ultimate male. But that was before she discovered Eric Parker.

Jessica snatched the application from Elizabeth and added candy-striper and baby-sitter. Still, the list looked somewhat skimpy. "I'm just going to have to get some new interests," she decided.

"Between now and Friday?" Elizabeth asked.

"Yep!"

"Jess, I wouldn't worry about it so much. Eric Parker's looking for an *ordinary* high school student, remember?" Elizabeth reminded her.

Jessica shook her head. There was ordinary—and then there was *ordinary*. And it looked like being the right kind of ordinary to be chosen by Eric Parker was going to take a little more work than she had anticipated!

# Two

"I just don't know what to do," Jessica declared three days later as she dumped her bookbag next to the swimming pool in the Wakefields' backyard.

Elizabeth was lying on a beach towel she had spread on the white pavement, reading her history textbook. She rolled over to look at her twin and pushed her sunglasses up on her head. "What to do about what?"

Jessica sprawled dramatically on a lounge chair. "My application for Eric Parker's talk show. Tomorrow's the deadline, and I still haven't come up with a way to beef up my application without outright lying!"

Elizabeth grinned and picked up a section of

the daily paper, which she had been reading earlier. "Here's just the story for you: 'How to Become a Well-Rounded, Average American Kid Overnight!'"

"Go ahead and laugh," Jessica said, sighing in resignation. "I'm glad you're amused by my anguish."

"Poor Jessica," teased Elizabeth. "You're right, it does say right here on page two that the earth will stop turning if you don't win the spot on Eric Parker's TV program."

Jessica yanked off her sweatshirt and pushed aside the straps of her tank top in order to tan her shoulders. Elizabeth just did not understand. Elizabeth wasn't the one who had sneaked a peek at Lila's application at lunch that day, when Lila was away from the table buying a soda!

Jessica had stared in disbelief. Lila, who Jessica knew for a fact was the most spoiled, selfish, and lazy girl in the whole world, who had zero community spirit, and who had never held a job or participated in extracurricular activities, had fudged a list of pseudo-interests and involvements as long as Jessica's arm. She described herself as an amateur chef; Jessica guessed that had come from the time the two of them had taken a cooking class at the Sweet Valley Civic Center. Lila had been even more of a disaster in the kitchen than Jessica! And she certainly had never touched a dirty dish or cooking utensil at Fowler Crest.

But at least the chef story had *some* basis in reality. Jessica had no idea how Lila could have claimed to be a photographer! Had she once snapped a couple of Polaroids at a family party? And a tutor at school? *Lila* was the one who needed tutoring. Her grades were awful! Then she had had the nerve to mention her role as co-chair of the Sweet Valley Centennial Celebration picnic. Jessica, as the other co-chair, had done virtually all the work! But Lila had really launched into science fiction with her "plans for the future." She had talked as if she were going to change the world, when everyone knew she would just go on doing what she always did—sitting on her fanny and spending her father's money. And what Lila had neglected to mention on her application angered Jessica almost as much as what she had written. There was absolutely no hint of Lila's wealthy, privileged background or of the fact that she had been kicked off the cheerleading squad as punishment for a prank she had pulled.

Lila's application had infuriated Jessica—and also worried her. "If only I were a little more like you," she told Elizabeth now. "I mean, mostly like me, but with a little of your nerdiness thrown in for balance."

"Gee, thanks," Elizabeth remarked dryly.

"You know what I mean. You're a columnist for the school newspaper—that's just the sort of thing that would impress Eric Parker."

Elizabeth considered her sister's comment for a moment. Then her eyes lit up. "Hey, why don't *you* write an article for *The Oracle*?"

"Me?"

"Yes, you," said Elizabeth. "Penny's still looking for a special feature for the next issue." Penny Ayala was editor in chief of *The Oracle*. "In fact, she's starting to get desperate. We were just talking about it today. Maybe you should give her a call."

"Hey, Liz, that's a great idea!" Jessica leaped from the lounge chair and dashed into the house. A minute later she was back by the poolside with the cordless telephone. Quickly she punched in the number Elizabeth recited.

"Penny, hi, it's Jessica Wakefield. How are you? Well, actually my sister suggested I call. She said you were looking for an article for the newspaper, and I'd like to offer myself as a guest columnist."

Jessica shot a look at Elizabeth. "Um, my idea for a story?" *Think fast, Wakefield.* She tried to think of what she did best, and flirting and dating came to mind. Then inspiration struck. "Well, I thought I'd try my hand at some humor. How does 'The Worst Dates of My Life' sound?"

Penny laughed; so did Elizabeth. Jessica grinned. She did have a reputation as a social butterfly—she had probably been on more dates than any girl at Sweet Valley High. And she definitely had had her share of romantic disasters!

"I like it," Penny said. "Can you put something together tonight? Then we could look it over at school tomorrow and decide whether it would work for *The Oracle*."

"You're on!" Jessica turned off the phone and flashed a triumphant smile at Elizabeth. "Liz," she announced, "I'm borrowing your type-writer!"

Elizabeth stood in the Wakefields' Spanish-tiled kitchen, slicing vegetables for a big tossed salad. When she had checked on her twin a little earlier, almost two hours after she had flown upstairs to work on her article, Jessica had been typing energetically with two fingers, pausing every ten seconds or so to correct a mistake.

Suddenly Jessica burst into the kitchen, her

cheeks pink and her eyes bright. "Here!" she said, proudly presenting Elizabeth with three single-spaced, typewritten pages. "Take a look. This writing business isn't so hard after all!"

"So you're ready to take over my column?" Elizabeth joked.

"Just read it," Jessica urged. "I really want to know what you think."

Elizabeth took a seat at the kitchen table and began to read her sister's article. Jessica's very first sentence made her laugh out loud: "Whoever said 'Chivalry is dead' and 'It's a jungle out there' must have had the Sweet Valley High dating scene in mind." In fact, Elizabeth didn't stop laughing all the way through.

"You have had some truly awful dating experiences, Jess! And you hit just the right comedic tone," she said with admiration. Elizabeth was genuinely surprised and impressed—she could not have written a better article herself. "It's funny, biting—perfect satire!"

Jessica shrugged. The literary critique meant nothing to her; she was more interested in the entertainment factor. "What part do you like best?"

"The part about the longest date of your life, with Winston on the deserted island, is good. But I think the funniest of all are your computer-dating-service disasters," answered Elizabeth, chuckling again as she recalled her sister's stories. "Scrawny Spence Millgate with glasses three inches thick and his dream of becoming an undertaker. And John Karger, the guy you met through the personal ad, who turned out to be studying you for a sociology project!"

"I didn't laugh at the time," admitted Jessica, "but it makes a funny story now."

"I notice that you didn't say anything about the reason behind your getting stuck with so many rotten blind dates. Don't you think people would love to hear about your signing yourself up at a dating service? And about the fake personalities you invented, Magenta Galaxy and Daniella Fromage?" teased Elizabeth.

Jessica grinned. "Poetic license, right?"

"But are you sure . . ." Elizabeth paused as she glanced back through the article for a particular paragraph. "Are you sure you should include this part about Bruce Patman?"

It had been months since Jessica's last date with Bruce Patman, the richest and most conceited boy at Sweet Valley High, but Jessica still got a sour taste in her mouth when she thought about having gone out with him—and about having made such a fool of herself. "Why not?" she asked. "It's the truth!"

" 'The worst dates are with the type of guy who thinks wearing too much expensive cologne and throwing around a lot of money can make up for the fact that all he does is talk about himself. Bruce Patman falls into this category,' " read Elizabeth. " 'I thought it would be fun to go parking in his black Porsche—until I discovered he kisses like a dead jellyfish!' " Elizabeth giggled in spite of herself. The anecdote about Bruce was mean, but it was also hilarious. Elizabeth couldn't resist asking, "Does Bruce *really* kiss like a dead jellyfish?"

Jessica shrugged. "I have to admit I took a few liberties with that description. But he deserves it."

"Well, Bruce isn't my favorite person, but I still think you should tone down his part a bit," Elizabeth said. "First of all, writing nasty things that aren't true about people is called libel."

Jessica rolled her eyes. "Oh, Liz, you take everything so seriously!"

"Well, it *is* serious," Elizabeth protested. "We're talking about journalistic ethics."

"It's just one little article," said Jessica.

"One little article can have lots of big repercussions," her sister pointed out. "Besides, I'm not the only one who will warn you. Penny will tell you the same thing. I mean, think about it, Jess. The entire school is going to be reading this article."

Jessica smiled devilishly. "Exactly! Admit it, Liz, it's no more than Bruce deserves."

"Well, then at least change his name," Elizabeth suggested. "You can still make your point and you'll keep yourself out of trouble at the same time."

"Maybe you're right," Jessica reluctantly agreed. "OK. Will you help me revise it? I'll change anything to make sure that Penny prints my article!"

On Friday Jessica and Elizabeth stopped by the newspaper office during lunch period. Jessica held her breath as Penny read "The Worst Dates of My Life." Jessica had made most of the changes her sister recommended—but not all. She had blurred some of the details and had given all the Sweet Valley High boys silly, phony names that only hinted at their real identities. Winston Egbert had become Kevin Klutz, Bruce was dubbed Reginald Rich, and so on. It would be entertaining, Jessica thought, to see just how long it took *The Oracle*'s readers to figure out who was whom. Penny was the first real test.

And so far, Penny was laughing even harder than Elizabeth had. "It's terrific, Jessica,"

Penny said at last. "Liz, I didn't know your sister shared your flair for writing!"

"I didn't either," Elizabeth said without much enthusiasm.

"It took us both by surprise," Jessica said breezily. "Everyone just *assumed* Liz had a corner on the literary talent in our family."

"One thing though, Penny," Elizabeth said. "Don't you think Jessica should try a little harder to disguise the boys' identities? Reginald Rich in particular?"

Penny's hazel eyes crinkled in a smile. "Not really, but it's up to her. The article's fine by my standards, and what makes it so funny is that we know these are Sweet Valley guys and we can try to guess who they are—although it isn't hard. Still, it's up to you, Jess. If you're prepared to deal with a few offended egos, I'd leave it. It's perfect as it is."

" 'Perfect as it is,' " repeated Jessica, pleased with herself. "Hear that, Liz?"

Elizabeth had heard. *Perfect as it is*—Elizabeth couldn't recall that Penny had ever said that about any of *her* articles.

"I can deal with bruised male egos," Jessica said with a sly grin. "Besides, I like stirring things up."

"Then I'll definitely use the piece." Penny squeezed Jessica's arm. "Thanks for coming through for me. I'll send your article to the typesetter today with the rest of the material for the next issue!"

"Great!" exclaimed Jessica. "And let me know if you ever need another special feature. I have a few more ideas that you just might like!"

"Will do," Penny assured her. " 'Bye, you two."

They had hardly passed through the door of the *Oracle* office when Jessica whipped the *Eric Parker Show* application out of her notebook. Resting the sheet against the wall, she quickly added "Feature writer for school newspaper" to the list of her interests and activities. "Now I'll be picked for sure!" she declared.

Elizabeth followed as Jessica hurried to the main office to submit her application.

"I can't believe he'll be right here in Sweet Valley in less than twenty-four hours!" breathed Jessica. "Eric Parker in the flesh!"

"I for one can't wait," Elizabeth said seriously.

"You can't?" Enid Rollins, Elizabeth's best friend, was surprised.

"I can't wait until Eric Parker gets here and

picks somebody to be on his TV show and puts an end to all this fuss," Elizabeth elaborated.

Todd nodded his head. "I agree. I'm ready for a new topic of conversation at school."

It was Monday evening, and the four were sitting at the picnic table by the Wakefields' pool eating take-out Chinese food. Mr. and Mrs. Wakefield both were working late; they had phoned to tell the twins to go ahead and have dinner without them.

"You mean you don't even care whether I'm chosen or not?" Jessica asked, sounding hurt.

"Of course I care, Jess," Elizabeth assured her. "I think you'd be a great representative of Sweet Valley High, and when Eric Parker reads your application, I bet he'll think the same."

Elizabeth wasn't just trying to flatter her twin; she meant what she said. Jessica had really put together a fantastic application. In fact, Jessica's efforts had started Elizabeth thinking. Maybe *she* was the one who wasn't well-rounded enough.

"I wonder what kind of application I could have put together for Eric Parker," Elizabeth said now. "Not that I wanted to be on TV, but even if I had, too many of my extracurricular activities are literary—my column for *The Oracle*, doing feature articles, writing poetry, keeping a journal."

"But you like being literary," Jessica pointed out as she picked up a piece of shrimp with her chopsticks.

"You're going to be a famous writer someday," Enid reminded her.

"That's what I've always thought I wanted. But . . ." Elizabeth paused. *But maybe I don't have what it takes*, she had been about to say. Elizabeth remembered what a hard time she had had recently getting a successful interview out of Claire Middleton. As it turned out, the problem had been Claire's and not her own; Claire had been going through a difficult time and was reluctant to talk to anyone. Still, Penny Ayala's praise of Jessica's writing the other day had rankled Elizabeth more than she wanted to admit. Penny never gushed over Elizabeth's weekly "Eyes and Ears" column or even about any of her feature articles.

*Maybe I'm losing my touch*, Elizabeth thought. What was the point, anyway, of being the supposedly literary twin if Jessica could write just as well as she could? And she made it seem so easy!

Elizabeth realized that Jessica, Enid, and Todd were still waiting for her to finish her sentence. "But . . . oh, I don't know. Maybe I've settled on a career path too soon," she concluded somewhat lamely.

"Would you rather have absolutely *no idea* what you want to be when you grow up?" her twin asked seriously. Jessica had hedged on the "Plans for the Future" question on the application. She had made a bit of a joke out of it, writing that she was still deciding among various possibilities, which included being a lawyer, an actress, an astronaut, and of course, President of the United States.

"There might be a happy medium," Elizabeth replied earnestly. "Like what you were saying the other day, Jess. About how you wished you were just a little bit more like me. Well, sometimes I wish I were just a little bit more like you. You're not afraid to try new things. You wrote for the newspaper, and you were a total success!"

"Beginner's luck," Jessica said modestly.

"No, it was more than that. There's something to be said for the way you approach life."

"I do like to experiment," agreed Jessica.

"I guess what I'm wondering is how I know there's not something out there I'd like more than writing?" *And something I'd be better at,* Elizabeth added silently.

Todd put a hand on Elizabeth's upper arm, playfully testing her muscle tone. "A little flabby," he teased. "Maybe you're too much of a bookworm. You need a sport to balance you out."

"Just don't do anything nutty like you did that time you took up surfing," interjected Enid.

"How about trying out for the Sweet Valley High girls' basketball team?" suggested Todd. "I'd be more than happy to give you a little private coaching." He bent forward to brush her cheek with a kiss. "Maybe some one-on-one . . ."

"Give me a break," said Jessica, then groaned. "As if you two don't already dribble enough over each other!"

Elizabeth smiled at Todd. "Let me remind you, Hotshot Wilkins, that I couldn't sink a basket to save my life. And I don't have time to practice with a team every day after school—I could only spare a few afternoons a week at this point. Besides, a sport isn't quite what I had in mind. Like Enid said, I've tried that already." She narrowed her eyes thoughtfully. It wasn't easy to express the vague feelings she was having. "I'm talking about more than just trying something new. Maybe I should start thinking about a different career, at least branch out a little."

Todd raised his eyebrows. "Sounds drastic, Liz."

"Well, why not?" she countered. Suddenly she felt sure of herself. "There are more important things in life than writing. Like the environment. Dad talked a lot about conservation issues during his mayoral campaign. He got me interested in the subject."

"She has me scrubbing out Prince Albert's dog food cans for recycling," Jessica confirmed, wrinkling her nose.

Enid leaned forward, her elbows on the table. "You know, that reminds me of something I read in the paper today. There's a new program starting up at Secca Lake. The park's recruiting high school students to volunteer as junior rangers and tour guides. I was thinking about dropping in at the first meeting tomorrow night, just to check it out. Why don't you come with me, Liz?"

Elizabeth considered Enid's proposal. "Volunteering at Secca Lake—that's kind of a neat idea."

"You can read about it yourself. I tore out the article," Enid explained. "It's in here somewhere." She shuffled through her tote bag and finally pulled the article out. "Here it is." Enid handed it to Elizabeth.

" 'Junior rangers will lead nature walks, educate visitors about Secca Lake's ecosystem and the threat of pollution, and organize craft workshops for children,' " Elizabeth read out loud. "That does sound like fun."

"It wouldn't hurt to investigate," said Todd.

"Come with me to the meeting," Enid urged.

"I think I will," Elizabeth decided. "Being a junior ranger could be a real challenge. I mean, anyone can *write*."

"That's not true," Todd said earnestly. "Not everybody can write as well as you."

"I don't know about that." Elizabeth glanced at Jessica, who was happily polishing off the last of the egg roll. Elizabeth had always considered her creative talent above average, but perhaps she had been wrong; maybe it was not so special after all. No, she wouldn't just sit back and write about the world—she would go out there and get involved.

# Three

"Here comes the part about Eric Parker. Everybody shut up!" Lila commanded.

After school on Tuesday, a rowdy group of Sweet Valley High students was gathered in the entertainment room at Fowler Crest for an informal party celebrating Eric Parker's arrival in town. The talk show host had flown in that afternoon from New York City, where his program was usually taped.

A local news program was showing highlights of Eric Parker's gala reception at the mayor's office. Jessica popped the top on a can of soda, her eyes glued to the big-screen TV. "Just take a look at that man." She sighed, imagining what it would be like to gaze into his eyes, face to face.

Amy took a pretzel from the bag Cara Walker held out to her. "Maybe I should have filled out an application after all," she admitted.

Jessica sighed again. Eric Parker looked especially wonderful on the big screen—even better than when she watched his show on her own family's TV. Jet black hair swept back from a high forehead, smoky gray eyes set in a chiseled, sun-bronzed face—and what a smile! How could anybody's teeth be so white? Jessica wondered.

"The mayor's really bending over backward," observed Cara, a good friend of Jessica's who dated the twins' older brother, Steven, a freshman at the nearby state university.

"Filming a show here is great PR for Sweet Valley," Bill Chase pointed out. "It's just good politics to give the guy the key to the city and all that."

"I wish it was the key to my house," Lila said rapturously.

"So do I," declared Jessica. "Then he'd see where you live and realize that your application is a bunch of baloney and that you're not Little Miss Average after all!"

Lila gave Jessica a cool, superior look. "Do I detect a trace of anxiety, Jess? Afraid Eric Parker's not going to give your feeble application a second glance?"

"I'm not in the least bit anxious," Jessica swore. She wasn't either. But she *was* angry about Lila's outrageously false application for the guest spot on the special broadcast.

Before the news had come on, they had all compared notes about their applications. From what Jessica could tell, nobody else's was as solid as hers. Her fellow cheerleaders like Robin Wilson, Maria Santelli, and Cara were not all that well-rounded. Ken Matthews and Aaron Dallas were just jocks; Aaron's girlfriend, Dana Larson, lead singer for the rock band The Droids, was a little too wacky. Surfer Bill Chase was too Californian, and *his* girlfriend, DeeDee Gordon, was too arty. No, none of her friends came across as well-balanced or as interesting as she did—of that Jessica was certain. Only Lila appeared to pose a threat, and that was only because of her padded application.

"You can't deny it, Li," pressed Jessica. "I saw your application at lunch the other day. It didn't exactly portray the real you."

Lila crossed her heart and smiled apologetically. "I didn't tell a single lie."

"Maybe not, but you exaggerated like crazy, and you left out a lot of stuff. That's the same as lying!" Jessica protested.

"What did she leave out?" Cara asked curiously.

"She conveniently forgot to mention that her dad's a multimillionaire who practically owns the town of Sweet Valley," Jessica informed Cara and the rest of the group. "And what about your zillion and one vacations to Europe and the Caribbean?" she demanded of Lila.

Lila shrugged. "I said I liked to travel. I just didn't say how often I actually *do* travel. And the application didn't ask me to list my father's assets."

Bill laughed. "She's got you there, Jess."

Jessica stuck her tongue out at him. "Who asked you, Bill?"

Lila abandoned defense for offense. "You know, I think this is a case of—what's that cliché?—the pot calling the kettle black," she countered. "Who's the one claiming to be a feature writer for the school newspaper all of a sudden? I, for one, am highly skeptical."

"It's the absolute truth. Ask Penny Ayala! My article will be in the next issue of *The Oracle*." Jessica smiled slyly. "And believe me, you won't be able to overlook it."

"It still sounds kind of cheesy to me," Lila complained. "One wimpy article, and all of a sudden you're passing yourself off as Jessica

34

the Journalist. You probably had Liz write it for you, didn't you?"

"How dare you—"

Aaron interrupted their squabbling. "Shh. Eric's making a speech."

The handsome celebrity was squarely facing the camera. For a moment, Jessica forgot about Lila's unjust accusation. She was conscious only of the way Eric Parker's magnetic gray eyes seemed to be looking right into hers.

"Nothing could make me happier than this warm welcome back to my beautiful hometown," Eric declared. His rich, deep voice sent a tingle up Jessica's spine. "I enjoy life in the Big Apple, but I've got to say, Sweet Valley still holds first place in my heart. I'm looking forward to spending ten days in sunny Southern California. This Friday, we'll be taping the show live from Hollywood."

"Get to the point!" Lila barked impatiently at the TV.

"And a week from Friday," Eric continued, "we'll broadcast live from my own alma mater, Sweet Valley High. This town has good reason to be proud of its young people. I've already begun reviewing the applications submitted by students vying for the guest spot on my program, and I can see it's going to be very difficult to choose just one. And because I want to announce a winner tomorrow morning, I'd better return to my hotel and get back to work!"

Eric Parker's face was abruptly replaced by a weather map. Lila flicked off the TV with the remote control. With another push of a button, she turned on the stereo system, indicating that everyone present was to shift into party mode.

Jessica hopped up from the couch and bounced over to the table where the Fowlers' maid had arranged soft drinks and snack food. She couldn't sit still knowing that Eric Parker was on his way back to his hotel and that he would soon be reading her application.

Squeezing her eyes shut, Jessica sent a fervent message to Eric Parker: *Choose me, Eric! Please choose me!*

There were a number of cars parked in the lot by Secca Lodge that evening when Elizabeth and Enid pulled up in the red Fiat convertible Elizabeth shared with her twin. As they got out of the car, both girls were struck by the beauty of the setting sun, which was causing the surface of Secca Lake to glimmer like molten gold.

Elizabeth thought of all the fun she had had with her friends and family at Secca Lake over the years: the picnics, the swims, the moonlit nights when she and Todd would drive around to the far shore of the lake to be alone with the silence of nature and each other. It was a special place.

Suddenly Elizabeth was very glad Enid had told her about the junior ranger meeting. It could lead to a meaningful involvement in a worthwhile cause; it could give her a whole new outlook on the world. *I could make a difference*, Elizabeth thought.

"I love the lake," Enid said to Elizabeth as they entered the community room of the lodge, which also housed changing rooms and a snack bar. "I'd love to help preserve it so that Sweet Valley can enjoy it forever."

"Me, too," Elizabeth agreed. "And it looks like we're not the only people who feel that way."

About two dozen teenagers had already gathered in the lodge for the meeting. Elizabeth and Enid were just in time. As soon as they were seated at one of the rough-hewn tables, a tall young man in jeans and a work shirt stood up and faced the group.

His tanned face creased in a friendly smile. "I've got to say, I'm really pleased by this great turnout. I'm glad to meet so many kids who are willing to take time to work for the park."

Enid nudged Elizabeth with her elbow. "He's pretty cute," she whispered.

"Cute—and taken," Elizabeth whispered back. "Note the gold band on the ring finger of his left hand."

Enid pretended to be disappointed. "Aw, shucks!"

"Before we get talking about the junior ranger program, I want to do the old go-around-the-room-and-introduce-yourself routine," he continued. "Only fair for me to start. I'm Don Wolff, and I've been a ranger at Secca Lake since I graduated three years ago from the University of California with a degree in forestry. My particular interest is environmental education, which is why I've been put in charge of the junior ranger program. Now let's hear from you."

Elizabeth was impressed by how enthusiastic most of the students were. A few hoped to use the Secca Lake training to prepare for summer jobs at state parks or with environmental organizations.

Elizabeth and Enid were the last to speak. "I'm Enid Rollins, and I'm a junior at Sweet Valley High," Enid began, smiling shyly. "I'm not an Eagle Scout or anything, but I like outdoor activities. I like the idea of getting a tan and doing something educational at the same time!"

The other kids laughed. Now it was Elizabeth's turn. "My name's Elizabeth—Liz—Wakefield, and I go to school with Enid. I've spent a lot of time at the park, but I'll admit I don't know much at all about how things happen behind the scenes. I'm eager to learn, though."

"And that's all I ask," said Don, giving her an encouraging smile. "You guys provide the desire and the energy, and I'll provide the experience. The goal is to make an informed conservationist out of each of you, and through you to reach the other people, old and young, who come to the park. Through tours and workshops we'll work to get the word out about what the community at large can do to help preserve the natural resource of Secca Lake."

Don walked over to some large cardboard boxes in the corner of the room. Reaching into the first box, he pulled out a khaki shirt and a pair of trousers. "These are the ranger uniforms, tops and bottoms." From another box, he drew a bright, flame-colored jacket. "I'll distribute the uniforms next time. I have to warn you all, though—they're not just for show.

Before you get to wear one, you have to earn it."

From a third box, Don grabbed a handful of little booklets. "Park rules and safety procedures," he explained as he passed them around. "You'll have two days to memorize them. We'll meet here again Thursday evening, same time, and there will be a quiz on the information in these booklets."

Somebody groaned, and Don grinned. "Being a junior ranger will be fun, but it's also an important responsibility. For that reason, only those who score one hundred percent on the quiz will move on to the next phase of training—an all-day park orientation that will be held this Saturday."

"One hundred?" repeated a sandy-haired boy at Elizabeth and Enid's table. "Isn't that a little stiff? Everybody makes mistakes sometimes."

"Just make sure one of those times isn't when you're taking the quiz," advised Don good-naturedly. "Any more questions? No? See you on Thursday, then."

The moon had risen while Elizabeth and Enid were in the lodge. It was a breathtaking night. Instead of getting into the car, the two girls headed to the lakeshore.

Enid took off her sandals so that she could

walk barefoot in the sand. "So what do you think?"

"It sounds like it'll be a challenge."

"Right up your alley, I'd say," said Enid. "You'll ace the quiz, no problem. I'm not so sure about my chances, though."

"You'll do fine," Elizabeth predicted. "I found Don's talk inspiring."

"I found Don inspiring," kidded Enid.

Elizabeth skipped a stone across the calm surface of the lake. She was already planning to dash off her weekly gossip column for *The Oracle* so that she would have more time to prepare for the quiz. She did not want to risk getting a single answer wrong and having her junior ranger career end before it had even begun. "The park, and the whole issue of conservation, is so important," she said with conviction. "I'm really excited about becoming a part of the movement, aren't you?"

"Ready to change the world already, Liz?"

Elizabeth joined in her friend's laughter, but she was serious. She was excited about the program. She realized that it had been a long time since her writing had made her feel as alive as she felt at that moment. She had come to this meeting tonight almost on a whim. She had been looking for a way to grow, for a new direction in which to head, and now she had found one. She could not wait to get started! And she could not help but wonder if volunteering for the park service would replace her first love.

# Four

"Where did you get that gorgeous photo of Jamie Peters?" Lila said with a gasp.

"This month's *Flipside* magazine," answered Jessica. "I can't believe you didn't see the article! His new album is coming out really soon. It's supposed to be his best yet."

It was Wednesday morning before school, and the two girls were gazing raptly at the glossy picture taped inside Jessica's locker. The legendary rock star stared back out at them, his long hair tossed back over his shoulders and a sexy half-smile on his rugged face.

"It can't be any better than the last one," Lila said. "I haven't stopped playing that CD since I bought it."

"Tell me about it." Jessica laughed. "I've driven everybody at my house crazy playing that one song, 'Barefoot Girl,' over and over again!"

"I love that one," Lila agreed, kissing her fingers and then touching them to the picture of Jamie Peters. "I like to pretend he's singing about me."

"But he can't be singing about you," Jessica pointed out, "because he's singing about *me*!"

Lila frowned, and for a moment Jessica thought she was about to argue. But when Lila turned to face her, she laughed.

Jessica dug a notebook out of the mess at the bottom of her locker, then slammed the metal door shut.

"Did the story in *Flipside* say anything about when Jamie's going to start touring for the new album?" asked Lila.

Jessica shook her head. "No concert dates yet. But he's got to come to Southern California. Where else is he going to find so many barefoot girls?"

"So many barefoot girls who are ready to lay themselves at his feet and become his love slaves," Lila added with a sly smile.

While the two girls were talking, the hallway had become crowded with students waiting for the first-period bell to ring. But instead of the sound of the bell, the students were startled by the voice of the principal, Mr. Cooper, nicknamed "Chrome Dome" because he was virtually bald. The principal's voice crackled over the loudspeaker. "Students, may I have your attention, please. I have a special announcement to make. Eric Parker presented me with an envelope just a few moments ago." Jessica and Lila, who had been leaning against the lockers, stood up straight.

"A few moments ago?" Jessica said in surprise. "But the winner isn't supposed to be announced until lunchtime!"

"Because there were so many outstanding applicants for the guest spot on his program," Mr. Cooper continued, "Mr. Parker has opted to hold preliminary interviews with six students before making a final decision. The preliminary interviews will be held after school on Friday, and a winner will be announced on Monday."

Lila grabbed Jessica's arm. "Six of us!" she shrieked. "He's going to interview six of us!"

Jessica held her breath.

Mr. Cooper cleared his throat. "The six finalists are . . . Jessica Wakefield—"

"That's me!" screamed Jessica, leaping into the air with jubilation.

"Way to go, Wakefield!" exclaimed a couple of students who had paused nearby to listen to the announcement.

Jessica beamed joyfully at Lila. Lila frowned in return. *Some best friend,* Jessica thought. *That's the second nasty face this morning. Lila could at least try to look happy for me.*

As Mr. Cooper read through the rest of the list at a painfully slow pace, Lila's scowl deepened. "Winston Egbert . . ."

"Winston! No way!" Jessica giggled. "Ha, that's a funny one! Wait till Eric Parker meets *him.*"

". . . Olivia Davidson, Patty Gilbert, Jim Roberts . . ."

"Jim Roberts?" Jessica wrinkled her forehead. She wasn't sure she even knew who Jim Roberts *was.*

By now, Lila's expression was positively murderous, her body tense with frustration.

". . . and Lila Fowler," concluded the principal.

A self-satisfied, ear-to-ear grin spread across Lila's face. Jessica gave another exuberant bounce. "Li, we both made it!"

The girls threw their arms around each other and whirled in a giddy circle. Suddenly they stopped cold and stepped apart. Jessica eyed

Lila; Lila eyed Jessica. Jessica felt her elation deflate.

"So who's our competition again?" asked Lila coolly.

"Winston, Patty, Olivia, and Jim Roberts," Jessica recited.

Lila ticked them off on her fingers dismissively. "School clown, dancer, arts editor, photography buff. A classic bunch of nerds."

Jessica had to agree. Sure, they were all nice people, but someone as cool as Eric Parker was bound to recognize that each one was missing something crucial. He might want to feature a typical American student on his show, but he would also want the student to have some flash and sparkle. Jessica was confident that *she* could provide the sparkle. But she also knew that Lila could provide the flash.

"Nothing to worry about there," Lila predicted. She crossed her arms. Her expression had turned to stone. "It looks like it's going to come down to you and me."

Lila was right. Only a few minutes ago, she and Lila had been gushing about Jamie Peters's new album. But this was not the same Lila. Jessica knew that she was now looking at a hard-hearted competitor, not a friend. They had both survived the first skirmish, but the battle wasn't over yet. It had just begun!

*　　*　　*

That afternoon Elizabeth and Enid stopped by the library on their way to lunch. By the time they arrived at the cafeteria, there wasn't an empty table in sight.

"We could try outside," Enid suggested.

"I really need to study the Secca Lake rules book, though," said Elizabeth. "If we sit outside, I'll be tempted to sunbathe instead. Not that it isn't just as distracting in here," she added. The noise level in the cafeteria was pretty intense.

"Well, there's your sister and her friends." Enid nodded toward a table by one of the big windows. "It looks as if they have a few empty chairs at their table."

Balancing their trays carefully, Elizabeth and Enid made their way to the table Jessica was sharing with Cara, Amy, and Lila. The three girls were Jessica's closest friends, and she had lunch with them almost every day. But that day something was different about the otherwise familiar scene. Elizabeth could feel the tension as she approached. *Something's wrong with this picture*, she thought as she set down her tray.

"Hi, everybody," she said cheerfully.

"Hi, Liz," said Amy. Cara gave her a smile. Lila and Jessica, who were sitting on opposite sides of the table, grumbled hellos without looking in Elizabeth's direction. *Afraid they might end up looking at each other by accident*, Elizabeth figured. She exchanged a glance of amusement with Enid; she had a hunch she knew what this was all about.

Elizabeth looked toward Cara and Amy. "So you two must feel pretty privileged, being best pals with two potential celebrities."

"Yeah, it's a real privilege." Amy rolled her eyes heavenward. "We're all just bubbling over with joy."

"It could be fun," Cara said pointedly, "if certain people didn't take it all so *seriously*."

"Well, I'm proud of you, Jess." Elizabeth patted her twin on the back.

Jessica did not look at her twin. "I'm proud of myself," she said airily in the direction of the next table. "I think Eric Parker picked good finalists. With *one* exception. Too bad he didn't see through the utterly falsified application of one particular person. Too bad he has no way of knowing that one particular person neglected to mention several essential facts about herself and that she just isn't what she seems, eh, Cara?"

'Well, Jessica, I wouldn't say—"

"Yes, it's too bad he has no way of knowing," Lila interrupted, her voice dripping with

49

sarcasm, "how one person completely magnified her achievements. How one person advertised herself as a journalist after writing one measly article for the school newspaper, an article that nobody's even seen yet. Don't you think that's fairly slimy, Amy?"

"I don't know if *slimy*'s the word I'd use, Lila—"

Jessica twisted in her seat to glare at the side of Lila's averted head. "I didn't put a single thing on my application that wasn't true!" she cried.

Lila threw Jessica a cutting look over her shoulder. "Neither did I!"

Elizabeth opened her carton of apple juice. "I guess it's a good thing Eric Parker's holding these preliminary interviews," she observed. "This way he'll discover that *some* of the applicants for the TV spot are more mature than others."

"Yeah, really!" Cara declared in exasperation. "C'mon, Jess, c'mon, Lila. Don't you two think you're getting a little carried away over this? I mean, you don't see anyone throwing themselves off cliffs because they didn't get picked. After all, it's just a TV show."

"Just a TV show?" Jessica snapped her fingers briskly. "Wake up, Cara! This is the chance of a lifetime! Maybe you're content to be a nobody for the rest of your life, but I have ambitions. Being on Jeremy Frank's show is just the first step for me. This time I plan to go all the way!"

"OK, OK, so maybe it *is* a big deal," Cara conceded. "All I'm saying is, you could try to keep things in perspective."

"I have things in perfect perspective," Jessica assured her. "I have a perfect perspective on who deserves to be on Eric Parker's show."

"I do," Lila said.

"Wrong!" Jessica snapped. "I do!"

Cara threw up her hands in a sign of defeat. "Well, I tried."

Elizabeth shook her head. It really looked like war between Jessica and Lila. She was a little surprised that Jessica hadn't relented at all. Elizabeth knew her twin wanted very badly to be on *The Eric Parker Show*, but it was not like Jessica to lose her sense of humor entirely.

It was the Lila factor, Elizabeth decided, sipping her juice thoughtfully. If Jessica were with one of the other finalists, she'd probably be joking around and making light of the competition. But with Lila . . .

Everyone knew that Jessica and Lila were rivals as well as friends. Elizabeth could not begin to count the number of times the two had duked it out in the past over some cute boy.

Whenever Lila got a new outfit, Jessica felt compelled to run out and buy one, too, even if she could not afford it. And Elizabeth knew that Jessica had always felt a bit jealous of Lila's affluent, glamorous life-style. Elizabeth could tell that Jessica saw winning the guest spot on Eric Parker's show as a way of getting the better of Lila Fowler.

Elizabeth caught Cara's eye. "Well, the preliminary interviews are scheduled for Friday, and by Monday afternoon, it'll all be over."

"Thank goodness," Cara said. "I don't know how much more of this civil war I can take!"

# Five

After the last bell on Friday afternoon, Lila
made a beeline for the girls' room nearest her
locker. She dumped the contents of her snake-
skin pocketbook onto the counter by the mirror,
selected an eye pencil, a blusher, and a lipstick,
and set to work. A few minutes later, Lila
smiled at her touched-up reflection.

She'd used only subtle colors—nothing too
flashy. She looked soft, real . . . gorgeous!
*Maybe I should go for the natural look more often*,
Lila thought as she swept the cosmetics back
into her purse. But first, she would test out the
look on Eric Parker.

On her way out of the girls' room, Lila
passed Maria Santelli. "Good luck at your interview, Lila."

"Why, thank you, Maria," Lila said sweetly. *Good luck, my elbow*, she thought as she strolled down the hall in the direction of the conference room, where the interviews were to be held. Maria's boyfriend, Winston Egbert, was also up for the TV spot.

Each of the six final candidates for the guest spot on Eric Parker's talk show had drawn a slot for a fifteen-minute appointment that afternoon. Lila had drawn the first slot, which had made her happy until Jessica drew the last one. Which of them had the advantage now?

On the one hand, Lila would be the very first Sweet Valley High student Eric met—and first impressions were deep and lasting. On the other hand, Eric would wrap up the afternoon by spending some time with Jessica, and Lila knew her friend well enough to guess that Jessica would do everything in her power to make sure Eric forgot about everyone else he'd spoken with before. Especially her biggest competition—Lila.

*I'll come out on top*, Lila decided with confidence. Eric would be dazzled by her beauty and charm and wit—what man would not? The other students—even Jessica—were bound to seem bland and lifeless in comparison.

*Soon I'll be on TV*. Lila shared a smug smile with the empty hallway. It was only right, after all. The other kids—including Jessica, who had wormed her way onto television once by harassing poor Jeremy Frank when he was laid up with a broken leg—would not know how to deal with an opportunity like this. Whereas she, Lila, had been raised to know exactly what to do. She had been meeting famous people all her life. She knew how to handle herself in almost any social situation. She belonged on center stage.

The conference room was located on a side corridor next to the guidance and career counseling offices. Lila checked her watch. She was two minutes early—perhaps she had beaten Eric to the appointment. Being early was good strategy; she could select the seat that set her off to the best advantage.

Mr. Cooper's secretary was thumb-tacking a note to the conference room door as Lila approached.

"What's happened?" Lila inquired anxiously. "The interviews haven't been canceled, have they?"

"Oh, no, dear," the secretary assured her. "This note is just to inform the finalists that the location has been changed. The interviews will now be held in the auditorium."

Lila breathed a sigh of relief. She paused a moment to read the note the secretary had tacked up on the door. Then she turned on her heel and hurried back the way she had come.

On her way to the auditorium, she had an idea. A brilliant idea.

"It's been a pleasure talking with you, Lila," Eric Parker said warmly at the end of the meeting. "I'm sorry we had only fifteen minutes."

Lila treated him to a smile as bright as the Southern California sun. "Maybe we'll have a chance to talk again. In front of the television cameras," she added playfully.

Eric laughed, his famous ultrawhite teeth flashing. "We'll know soon. Thanks for your time, Lila."

"It was an honor," she assured him. " 'Bye!"

Lila had to restrain herself from kicking her heels together as she headed up the aisle to the auditorium exit. Just in case Eric was watching, she strolled with a pert but dignified step—a slight swing of the hips, nothing too seductive.

Once she was safely out of sight, Lila indulged in a little victory dance. The interview had been a breeze. She had fielded all of Eric's questions with humor and style and heartwarming sincerity. She could tell he had been impressed with her manner and her appearance. She had the TV spot in the bag! Her only real competition was Jessica, and she had thought of a way to get Jessica out of the running.

Lila's interview had begun at two-thirty. Jessica, the last candidate, was supposed to meet with Eric at three forty-five. Lila backtracked to the conference room and glanced quickly at the note still pinned on the door. Then she ducked into the career counseling office, pulled a book off the reference shelf, and made herself comfortable at one of the reading tables.

At twenty-five minutes past three, she re-shelved the book and peeked out the door into the corridor. Sure enough, here came Olivia Davidson, who was scheduled for the fifth interview. Lila watched as Olivia scanned the note on the conference room door and hurried away to the auditorium. Now Jessica was the only finalist who didn't know about the location change.

Lila stepped into the hallway. Casually, she approached the door to the conference room, and just as casually, she removed the note—thumbtack and all. Then, without a backward glance, she breezed through the lobby and out the front door of the school to the parking lot.

*Am I an absolute genius, or what?* In fifteen minutes, Jessica would arrive at the conference room. And because the note was gone, she would stay at the conference room. By the time

Jessica figured out where the interviews were actually being held, Eric Parker would be on his way back to his hotel room.

What a scheme—and it had been so easy! Lila revved the engine of her Triumph. She decided to go straight home and videotape herself talking about "Growing Up in America." She might as well start practicing for Eric Parker's program. With Jessica safely out of the running, Lila was sure she would win the spot, hands down.

She sped away from the school, the radio blasting. "Live from Sweet Valley High," she shouted out loud, "it's Lila Fowler!"

Jessica had been tempted to cut cheerleading practice and to spend the afternoon lurking in the vicinity of the conference room, spying on the other candidates as they met with Eric for their interviews. But finally she had decided that seeing Lila and the others would only make her nervous. So she had gone to cheerleading practice, but she had directed the others from the sidelines in order not to work up a sweat.

At quarter to four on the dot, Jessica arrived at the conference room, ready to knock Eric Parker's socks off. The door was closed. Wondering if Olivia, whose interview had been scheduled just before hers, was still with Eric, Jessica knocked lightly.

When she got no answer, she turned the knob and pushed open the door. The room was empty.

Two armchairs faced each other; a Styrofoam coffee cup sat on the table. Eric must have just ducked out for a break, Jessica thought as she seated herself in one of the chairs. *He'll be back in a minute.*

But when five minutes had passed and Eric still had not returned, Jessica began to panic. *I'm in the right place, aren't I?* she asked herself. *And it's the right day and the right time. . . . Yes,* she thought, *I was supposed to be at the conference room at three forty-five.* So what had gone wrong?

Suddenly a horrible thought occurred to her. Eric must have interviewed the other five contestants and liked one of them so much, he had decided not to even bother meeting Jessica!

No, that couldn't be. There had to be a reasonable explanation. Maybe somebody at the principal's office would know.

Jessica jumped up from her chair and dashed to the door of the conference room. As she burst into the hallway, she almost trampled Olivia Davidson.

"Jessica!" Olivia exclaimed in surprise. "What are you doing here?"

"What do you mean, what am I doing here?" said Jessica. "Weren't you here for the same reason twenty minutes ago? I'm waiting for my interview with Eric Parker!"

"But the interviews were moved to the auditorium," said Olivia.

Jessica's face went pale. "The auditorium?"

"Yes." Olivia frowned, puzzled. "That's funny. There was a note on the conference room door explaining the switch. That's how I knew where to go. Someone must have taken it down. You'd better get to the auditorium fast, Jess."

Sending a thank you to Olivia over her shoulder, Jessica sprinted off in the direction of the auditorium. But she might be too late. What if Eric Parker had already given up on her?

*I'm about to miss my interview with Eric Parker and blow my chance to be on national TV,* Jessica thought frantically as she skidded around a corner in the hall. *All because of a stupid note on a stupid door that some stupid person accidentally took down before I'd seen it.*

Or just maybe the person who had removed the note was not stupid, but devious and selfish and cruel! The suspicion quickly took root in Jessica's mind. Someone had tried to sabotage her interview. And Jessica had a pretty good idea who that someone was.

*I'll kill her*, Jessica thought grimly as she pushed open the heavy door of the auditorium. *This time that girl has gone too far. She'll pay for this!*

Jessica was overwhelmed with relief. Eric Parker was sitting on the edge of the stage. He was dressed in jeans and a polo shirt like any ordinary man, but he was looking twenty times more gorgeous than any ordinary man could ever be. Thank goodness he had waited for her!

"You must be Jessica," he said, hopping to his feet and extending a hand as she approached. "I'm Eric Parker."

Jessica shook his hand, her heart beating triple time.

"I'm really sorry I'm late," she apologized breathlessly. "There was a mix-up about the location. I guess I was the only one who didn't see the note saying that the interviews had been moved." Jessica laughed in spite of herself. "And for once I was going to be punctual!"

Eric glanced at her bare wrist. "Even without the help of a watch?"

"I never wear one," Jessica confessed. "As a rule, I let things happen when they happen."

"Well, are you ready for our interview to happen?" he asked with a smile.

"You bet!"

Eric gestured to a couple of folding chairs set up on the stage. "I decided to hold the interviews here because this is where the actual TV program will be taped," he explained.

They each took a seat, and Jessica waited expectantly.

"I enjoyed reading your application." Eric pulled Jessica's application from a manila folder that had been sitting on the floor by his chair. "Why don't we start by talking about something the application didn't cover?"

He was tossing the ball to her, Jessica realized. Well, she'd show him she could handle anything he sent her way. "Well, the form didn't allow me to write about the most important part of my life," she answered promptly, "my family."

"I'd love to hear about them now," Eric encouraged.

"We're pretty typical, I suppose. But lately, I've come to appreciate more than ever how lucky I am to be part of a strong, supportive family." Jessica faltered for a moment. Only a short time ago, when her parents had gone through a trial separation, she had come close to learning just how awful it would be to lose her family. Jessica sat up straighter in her chair and continued brightly, "My parents both work—Dad's a lawyer, and my mother has her own interior design business. My older brother Steven is in college now, but my sister Elizabeth's still around the house to bug me." She smiled, the dimple in her left cheek deepening. "Liz and I are identical twins. I don't suppose I'll ever get rid of her!"

Eric was interested. "I imagine being a twin has had quite an impact on your life."

"That's the truth," Jessica agreed. "I think a lot of people assume that twins are going to be exactly alike. Actually, I think that being a twin forces you to be even more of an individual than you might be otherwise. Liz and I are really close, but we do our own thing."

"It would be hard to say exactly what your thing is, Jessica, judging from your activity-packed application. It looks as if you have a lot of interests."

"I keep pretty busy," she said modestly.

"I see you were a candy-striper. What was that experience like?"

Actually, Jessica had hated being a candy-striper! She had only done it in order to meet Jeremy Frank; in general, catering to crabby hospital patients was not her idea of a good time. But Jessica had a feeling that in the present circumstances, the angel-of-mercy attitude would be more appropriate to take. "It was hard work but very rewarding," she fibbed. "Sick people really appreciate everything you do for them. They really respond to a friendly face." *That much is true, anyway,* Jessica thought. *I don't have to tell him that my face wasn't one of the friendly ones!*

All at once, Jessica was struck with a brilliant idea. Talking about candy-striping presented the perfect opportunity for getting back at Lila for having taken down that note!

"Yes, I'd volunteer again in a minute if I didn't have so many other things on my schedule these days," Jessica said. "I really enjoyed working at Joshua *Fowler* Memorial Hospital."

"Joshua Fowler," repeated Eric, taking the bait. "I interviewed a Lila Fowler earlier this afternoon. Any relation?"

"Is Lila back from Hong Kong already?" Jessica exclaimed. "It seems as if that lucky girl is never in school—she's always halfway around the world. Oh, yes," Jessica continued casually, "the Fowlers practically built the hospital and lots of other buildings in Sweet Valley too. In fact, they've given Sweet Valley so much money in the last few years, I wouldn't be surprised if someday the town's name is changed to Fowlerville! It must be nice to be rich enough to donate to good causes like hospitals and things."

"Hmm."

Jessica could see Eric making a mental note. Her heart bubbled up with vengeful delight. No doubt about it, Eric had gotten the picture. It was not your average family that had a hospital named after it! Consequently, Lila Fowler was not your average high school student. *Got you, Lila,* Jessica thought with satisfaction.

Eric resumed his questioning. "Did you volunteer as a candy-striper because you were considering a career in health care?"

Jessica knew that she couldn't very well answer honestly and say, "Not a chance." She quickly thought back to what Elizabeth had said about the positive side of Jessica's experimental attitude toward life. "To tell you the truth, Mr. Parker, at this point in my life, I'm still trying out different things, opening myself to new experiences. I figure I have some time to decide what it is I do best."

"You're exactly right," Eric said. "When I was your age, I thought I would go into business with my father. If I hadn't kept an open mind to other possibilities, I would never have found my niche in television."

"And I'm sure glad you did!" Jessica said.

Eric laughed. Then he glanced at his watch.

"Time flies when you're having fun. We've been chatting for twenty minutes."

They stood up, and Eric took Jessica's hand again and gave it a warm squeeze. "You're a very impressive young lady. I'm truly glad we met, and I hope we see more of each other during my stay in Sweet Valley."

"I hope so, too," Jessica said.

"So long, Jessica."

Jessica left the auditorium feeling as if she were floating on a cloud. Eric hoped to see more of her! That could only mean one thing—he was going to choose her to be on his show. Jessica was sure of it! The two of them had really clicked—Eric had to be thinking about how well they would work together on TV. And he also had to be wondering about Lila. Lila had probably buttered him up with her Miss Average America act, but now Eric knew the truth about the real Lila Fowler.

Jessica smiled. She couldn't wait to see Lila's face on Monday when Lila learned that her nasty trick had backfired.

# Six

"I'm so glad that we both scored one hundred on the quiz," Enid said as she climbed into the passenger seat of the Fiat on Saturday morning.

"Me, too," said Elizabeth warmly. "It's going to be fun being junior rangers together."

Enid rolled down her window, allowing the fresh breeze to tangle her curly brown hair. "And what a day to spend out by the lake!"

"It's absolutely gorgeous." Elizabeth turned onto the road that led to Secca Lake. "I'm going to feel a little guilty about enjoying myself at the park, though."

"Why?"

"Well, in order to do this ranger orientation, I had to give up an assignment for *The Oracle*,"

Elizabeth explained. "Penny wanted me to cover the student government fund-raiser this afternoon."

"Penny has other reporters," Enid reminded her friend. "And you'll get other assignments."

"True." Elizabeth sighed. "It's just that this is the first time in all the years I've worked on the newspaper that I've turned down an assignment. I just feel funny about it, that's all."

"You shouldn't," Enid insisted. "You do more than your share for *The Oracle*, and Penny knows it. I'm sure she's glad to cut you some slack for once."

Elizabeth knew that Enid was probably right. *Penny really doesn't seem to mind—but I do*, she thought. Elizabeth was not happy shirking her responsibility to the newspaper. But to be honest, she had not wanted to write about the fund-raiser in the first place. In fact, she did not feel much like writing about anything these days.

"Don't worry about Penny and the newspaper," Enid suggested as Elizabeth looked for a parking space at the lake. "*The Oracle*'s not your whole life. You should be celebrating—you made it into the ranger program! Isn't that what you wanted, to expand your horizons and be more well-rounded and all that?"

Elizabeth laughed. "Yes, it is. Thanks for

reminding me!" Enid was right. She was here to enjoy a beautiful day and to learn about conserving the environment. That was what was important right now.

Elizabeth and Enid found the other ten students who had been admitted into the junior ranger program inside Secca Lodge. They were trading their street clothes for ranger uniforms. Elizabeth noted with a grin that the sandy-haired boy who had complained about Don's one-hundred-percent rule was there. He must have gotten his act together enough to ace the quiz!

A few minutes later, the two girls emerged from the changing room. "Watch out, litterbugs," kidded Enid. "It's Ranger Wakefield."

Elizabeth shook a finger at her. "Don't feed the bears, if you know what's good for you!"

"C'mon." Enid started for the door. "Everybody else is already outside with Don."

"I hope you're ready for a long day," Don announced when the girls had joined the group and he had everyone's attention. "There's a lot of ground to cover, and I mean that literally. We'll start out by taking a tour of the park ourselves—we'll cover every foot of trail. I'll explain the trail-marking system as we go and identify some common plants, both poisonous and nonpoisonous. We'll also take a careful look at the lake itself. Pay close attention—you'll be leading your own nature walks soon. Finally, I'll review the history of the park—more information you'll need as tour guides. We'll finish up with some recreation—a swim and a snack. How does that sound?"

The new recruits unanimously expressed their enthusiasm. But by the end of the day, Elizabeth observed that some of the group were not as gung-ho as they'd been when they started out. She could understand why. By the time they had made a complete circuit of the trails around the lake and returned to the lodge, Elizabeth was tired and dusty. Her head was spinning with the names of what seemed like hundreds of different plants, birds, and animals. She had not realized there would be so much to learn! It was a pleasure to sink onto the sand. The other junior rangers collapsed on the beach.

"My muscles are going to be sore tomorrow," she predicted to Enid. "That was some hike! It was no mean feat just keeping up with Don."

"Tell me about it," Enid groaned. "I had no idea how out of shape I was. What a workout!"

"It was fun, though, wasn't it?" Elizabeth gazed out at the sun-dappled lake. "I liked learning how to mark and read trails. It's like knowing a secret code."

"I liked meeting the lifeguard staff," Enid said with a smile.

"I think they were impressed with you, too." Elizabeth winked at her friend.

"Speaking of being impressed, Don certainly was when you were the only one who knew that bit about Secca Lake being fed by a stream that passes through an industrial area and about how ten years ago Sweet Valley residents lobbied for a big cleanup. Their efforts actually helped make the lake safe for swimming again."

"I learned that when my dad was campaigning for mayor," Elizabeth reminded Enid. "He researched a lot of facts like that. It's a great story, isn't it?"

Don passed out soda and bags of chips to all the junior rangers. Then he sat down in the sand beside Elizabeth.

Elizabeth gulped down half the can in just a few swallows. "All of that walking sure made me thirsty! I'll have to get a flask for water like yours, Don."

"It's a necessity," he agreed. "So what do you two think about the junior ranger program so far? Are you going to stick it out?"

"I'm happier than ever that I decided to get involved," Enid told him.

"I feel like I'm seeing Secca Lake and the park in a whole new light," Elizabeth said sincerely. "We're so lucky to have a beautiful place like this in our town. I never thought about it as a natural resource—it was just a place to hang out and have a good time. Now I realize that Secca Lake needs preserving just like any other place of natural beauty."

"You're both going to make good volunteers, I can tell." Don smiled as he tore open a bag of potato chips. "You learn quickly, and you have the right attitude, which is just as important. In fact," he said pulling a clipboard out of his backpack, "I wanted to appoint one of the twelve junior rangers to be the informal chief of operations. Someone I can count on to help me coordinate your schedules—someone to call when I need a backup."

Enid and Elizabeth exchanged an excited glance. Was Don going to ask one of the two of them?

Don looked up from the clipboard. His gaze settled on Elizabeth. "How about it, Liz? Would you be willing to take on the extra responsibility?"

Enid elbowed Elizabeth in the side. Elizabeth's eyes widened. "Well, I don't—maybe. . . ."

Elizabeth was taken aback by Don's offer. Already, with the ranger program and school and the newspaper, she was stretching herself a little thin to take on any more responsibilities.

And Elizabeth knew that she couldn't accept the position from Don unless she was sure she could come through for him and for the program.

The offer was flattering, though. Don had singled her out from a dozen talented kids. It made her feel good. Elizabeth suddenly remembered the way Penny had gushed over Jessica's story at *The Oracle* the other day. When was the last time Penny had given a rave review to a piece of Elizabeth's writing?

*That doesn't really have anything to do with this,* Elizabeth told herself. Still, she could not deny that it felt great to have her abilities recognized. Don appreciated her; the park needed her. Why shouldn't she devote more of her time to the junior ranger project, even if it meant spending less time on her writing?

"Sure, Don," Elizabeth said cheerfully. "I'd be glad to."

"Great! OK, gang." Don raised his voice. "A little more work, then we can cut loose and hit the water. I'm going to ask you all to take on two shifts a week, one after school and one shift on the weekend. I need two people on Mondays—one for the four o'clock nature walk and one for the sunset tour. Who'll volunteer?"

As the junior rangers volunteered for shifts and Don took notes, Elizabeth sat down quickly.

"Lucky you, Liz, being made Don's assistant."

Elizabeth smiled at her friend's enthusiasm. Still, she could not help but wonder what she had gotten herself into: two shifts a week plus nature workshops and now extra duties at the park. It might not be long before she was forced to turn down another reporting assignment.

"Liz, I'm so nervous, I could scream!" Jessica gripped her twin's arm so tightly, it hurt.

"Let go of me!" Elizabeth yelped. "Really, Jess, you'd think you were up for an Oscar or something."

"That'll be next," Jessica said. "First I'm going to win this TV spot!"

An assembly had been called before the first class on Monday morning in order to make various announcements. Avoiding her own friends—specifically, Lila—Jessica had grabbed a seat next to Elizabeth and Todd. Now she craned her neck and found Lila in the crowd. She hadn't talked to Lila since last Friday, before the preliminary interviews. For all Lila knew, her note-stealing prank had worked, and Jessica had missed her appointment with Eric Parker. *She's in for the surprise of her life*, Jessica anticipated gleefully. *Maybe I should have sat*

*with her so I can see her face when Eric announces
I'm the one he's picked to be on his TV show!*

Jessica barely listened as Mr. Cooper made a few remarks about upcoming school events. But when he introduced Eric Parker, Jessica sat forward in her seat, her hands clasped tightly together. Several groups of students jumped to their feet, clapping and whistling.

Eric, looking as dashing as usual, waved for silence. Then, declining to use the microphone and podium, he stepped forward to the edge of the stage.

"It's great to be back at Sweet Valley High," he began. There were more cheers. "I'm sorry to say that not many of the teachers remember me—it's been nearly fifteen years since I graduated. But talking with some of you has helped me get back in touch with my own high school days. Thanks to you, I think I'm ready for my special, 'Growing Up in America.' To that end, how about a hand for my guest star"—Eric paused dramatically—"Miss Jessica Wakefield!"

*That's me*, Jessica realized, stunned. *He picked me!*

Her dream had come true, and she was paralyzed. "Get up there!" Elizabeth hissed. When Jessica still didn't budge, Elizabeth pushed her up out of her seat and into the aisle.

Jessica took a first awkward step. *He picked*

*me!* She didn't even feel the floor beneath her feet as she proceeded to the stage to shake Eric's hand. Even tripping over the microphone cord and nearly falling on her face didn't seem to faze her. She was still marveling. *He picked me!*

Eric shook Jessica's hand, then faced the auditorium. "It was a tough choice," he said. "I wish I could have featured all the applicants on the show. But I will bring one more special person to your notice. I'd like to ask Lila Fowler to serve as Jessica's alternate. If for any reason Jessica can't make the broadcast on Friday, Lila will take her place. Congratulations, Lila!"

An alternate? *Lila?* As the audience applauded once more, Jessica's deliriously happy smile widened. This victory was a hundred times sweeter than she had ever imagined it could be! Eric was actually inviting Lila onstage to congratulate her for coming in second!

As Eric shook her hand, Lila beamed as if being named runner-up had been her goal all along. But when Eric turned away from her, Lila's smile faded into a look of fury and jealousy.

Jessica savored the moment to the fullest. She'd beat out Lila fair and square. Lila would never be able to act superior again. Jessica was going to be a TV star!

*  *  *

Without giving away the role she had played in delaying Jessica's interview on Friday, Lila got the whole story from Amy after the assembly. So Jessica had made it to her appointment with Eric Parker after all!

But that didn't explain how Eric could have preferred Jessica over Lila. She seethed every time she remembered Jessica's gleeful, gloating grin onstage that morning.

Lila had successfully avoided Jessica after the assembly, but now that it was lunchtime, Lila supposed she would finally have to face her. She decided she would assume the upper hand and act totally happy for Jessica. She would not show one ounce of jealousy. That would shut Jessica up.

Jessica was seated at the center of an animated group at one of the first tables in the cafeteria. Lila could not very well pretend not to see Jessica, who was waving energetically in her direction.

Lila joined the group, pulled out a chair, and with a sweet smile launched into her graceful loser speech. "I want to tell you how happy I am for you, Jess—"

"I know, isn't it absolutely fantastic?" Jessica gushed, looking around the table for reconfirmation. Amy, Bruce, Aaron, Dana, and Cara all nodded like puppets. "I'm on cloud nine. Make that cloud nine hundred and ninety-nine. I can't *believe* I'm going to be on TV with Eric Parker!"

"It's great, Jess," Lila said dryly.

"Maybe I'll get discovered by a talent scout," Jessica continued. "Wouldn't that be awesome, Li?"

"Oh, yes. Just awesome."

"So what do you think—will my first offer be to star on a daytime soap opera or to act in a commercial, or do you think I'll get a movie offer right away?"

Jessica winked at the others, then turned her sparkling eyes on Lila. She was clearly reveling in Lila's humiliation. Lila felt her cheeks grow warm with anger. How dare Jessica rub it in like this in front of absolutely everyone!

*Keep your cool, Fowler!* she commanded herself. *They all know Jessica's trying to antagonize you. Don't let them see you sweat.*

"Maybe a TV commercial," Lila replied, her voice cool and even. "For something totally outrageous. Like dog food," she added, "or nasal spray."

Everyone but Jessica laughed, and for a second Lila imagined she had put her uppity friend in her place.

But Jessica was just taking a breath before delivering her next verbal dagger. "Of course, I'm sorry *you* can't be on Eric's show, too, Lila." Her voice was so sugary sweet that Lila had an urge to gag. "It's too bad that only one of us could win and that the other had to be the *alternate*."

Lila clenched her fists in her lap and resisted the urge to reach across the table and slap the self-satisfied look off Jessica's face.

For the remainder of the lunch period, Jessica chattered on about her amazing opportunity. Lila did her best to ignore her friend's blatant taunts, but by the end of the period, she had been pushed to the limit. *Whatever it takes*, Lila vowed, glaring at Jessica and wishing that looks could kill, *whatever it takes, I'm going to show Jessica Wakefield what an alternate is good for!*

Lila was determined. She would get the Eric Parker TV spot away from Jessica if it was the last thing she ever did.

# Seven

"This is really a big week for you, Jess," Elizabeth noted as the twins drove to school on Tuesday morning. "Yesterday you found out you won the guest spot on Eric Parker's talk show, and today your feature article comes out in *The Oracle*."

"I know. I can't wait to see it," her twin replied. "So step on it, Liz!"

"You *are* prepared, though," Elizabeth continued. "I mean, when this hits the halls and people figure out who's who in 'The Worst Dates of My Life'—"

"Liz, you know I changed the names to protect the not-so-innocent," Jessica reminded her. "So what if a couple of guys get mad? The rest of the school will be laughing their heads off."

Elizabeth was silent as she turned into the Sweet Valley High parking lot. She certainly hoped that her sister was right.

As usual, the hot-off-the-press editions of *The Oracle* were stacked in the main lobby of the school. In her eagerness to get her hands on a copy, Jessica practically knocked a skinny freshman off his feet. "Sorry," he mumbled in confusion.

Jessica ignored the blushing boy and flipped rapidly through the pages of the newspaper. "Here it is, Liz!" she shrieked with delight. "Page four. Right next to 'Eyes and Ears'! They look great together." Jessica scanned the first paragraph of "The Worst Dates of My Life" and giggled. "I forgot what a scream my article was!"

On an impulse, Elizabeth had asked Penny to print Jessica's article alongside her own regular column. Now, as she looked at the two pieces, she wished she had not had the idea of teaming up her journalistic efforts with those of her sister. Next to Jessica's spicy, irreverent anecdotes, "Eyes and Ears" seemed dry and uninspired.

"Your article is the funniest thing that's been printed in *The Oracle* all year," Elizabeth said, looking up from her own copy of the paper. *And it bothers me*, she had to admit to herself.

"Hey, Jessica!"

Jessica turned to see Ken Matthews waving a copy of *The Oracle* at her and grinning. "Guess I'm a pretty lucky guy—I didn't get mentioned in your story!"

"I thought I'd spare you for Terri's sake. I didn't want her thinking she'd hooked up with a bozo," she teased.

"Not everybody got off so easy, though," Ken observed. "I know one guy who's going to be pretty steamed."

"Who?" Jessica asked innocently.

"I won't mention any names . . ." Ken began.

"And neither did I," Jessica countered. "So no one has any reason to be offended."

Ken laughed as he turned to leave. "Tell that to Reginald Rich!"

As Jessica and Elizabeth walked to their lockers, Jessica was delighted to see that the hall was crowded with students scanning the newspaper—and laughing over what had to be her story. And every few feet, someone stopped her to comment on it.

"Hey, Jess, kissed any dead jellyfish lately?" Winston asked.

"Not since I washed up on that deserted island with you!"

"I could be mad at you, you know." Winston faked an elaborate scowl.

"I didn't say anything bad about *you*," Jessica

pointed out. "It was the circumstances that made it a 'worst date.' "

"Well, I've got to say, it's a hilarious article," Winston complimented her. "You're *almost* as funny as me, Wakefield!"

"Jessica!" Jessica turned to see Danny Stauffer, a boy she had dated a few times in the past. "I really liked your article."

Jessica fluttered her eyelashes. *I forgot how cute Danny is!* "Thanks, Danny."

"But I've got to tell you," he added, "I was thinking about giving you a call to see if you wanted to get together again. Now I'm not so sure it's a good idea. I don't want to end up a casualty of 'The Worst Dates of My Life, Part Two'!"

Jessica laughed lightly and waved at him as he walked away. But when she turned back to Elizabeth, her expression was anxious. "I didn't consider that angle, Liz. Do you think my article is going to scare away a lot of boys from asking me out?"

Elizabeth smiled and shook her head. Her twin had never had a problem getting dates, and Elizabeth seriously doubted she would start having a problem now. "I wouldn't sweat it, Jess. I'd like to see the day that boys stop calling you!"

Just then a cluster of sophomore girls strolled

by, their heads close together. Jessica heard one of them mention Bruce Patman's name, and no sooner had she done it than the others burst into wild giggles.

"Uh-oh, it sounds like the truth is getting around already!" Jessica was delighted at the idea of causing such a sensation. Her momentary anxiety seemed to be gone.

"What did you expect?" Elizabeth asked as she worked the combination to her locker. "You knew that changing the boys' names wasn't going to really hide their identities." Elizabeth removed her French textbook and slammed her locker shut. She lowered her voice dramatically. "Believe me, Jess, once everyone hears that the high-and-mighty Bruce Patman kisses like a dead jellyfish, it's going to be the talk of the town."

Jessica lifted her notebook to her face to hide her laughter. "If anyone in this entire school could use a dose of humility, it's Bruce. I think I deserve some kind of reward!"

"Hey, Jellyfish-lips! How about a smooch?" Neil Freemont called out down the hall.

Peter DeHaven, another tennis teammate of Bruce's, joined in the fun. "Had any good dates lately, Bruce—at the aquarium?"

"I'll nail you guys at practice," Bruce threatened. "And I'm going to nail you, too, Pfeifer," he shot at the boy walking by his side.

"Why me?" John Pfeifer asked. "I'm your buddy. You haven't heard me ribbing you."

The group was en route to an extra-credit afterschool science lecture for juniors and seniors. "Some buddy," Bruce grunted. "You're sports editor of the stupid *Oracle*, aren't you? Couldn't you have kept that asinine story out of the paper?"

John lifted his hands. "I'm innocent. I read over the sports page beforehand, and that's all. I swear, Patman, I had no idea that article was going to be in there." He grinned. "You've got to admit, though, it is pretty funny."

"I'd like to see Bruce admit that!" Todd whispered to Elizabeth as they passed alongside John and Bruce.

"I should write an article myself," Bruce snarled, loud enough for Elizabeth and Todd and everyone else in the hallway to hear him. "It's not like Wakefield was such a hot date herself."

"You'd have a hard time convincing anybody of that," John said. "She's one of the prettiest and most popular girls in school."

Though Bruce Patman was one of her least favorite people, Elizabeth actually felt sorry for him. All day long Bruce had been fair game for abuse from anyone who had read Jessica's article. And that was just about everyone in the entire school. He was probably relieved to take a seat in the classroom—at least his tormentors would have to shut up for the duration of the class!

Mr. Russo introduced the day's lecture, the subject of which was marine life. Mr. Russo flashed a slide of a marine invertebrate on the screen. Several students snickered in anticipation. "This is going to be good," Todd whispered. "Keep an eye on Patman!"

Mr. Russo's voice was loud and clear. "There is one free-swimming marine coelenterate we're all familiar with, if only from signs on the beach that warn us it's dangerous to swim when they've been spotted in the water." A girl in the back row giggled out loud. "Having a partially transparent, saucer-shaped body"—as Mr. Russo continued, the laughter in the room mounted—"and tentacles studded with stinging cells, this coelenterate's common name is the jellyfish."

No sooner had the word passed Mr. Russo's lips than the entire group, with the notable exception of Bruce Patman, doubled over with uncontrollable laughter.

John patted his friend on the back in sympathy. Though Bruce seemed to be doing his best to ignore the group's hilarity, from where she sat Elizabeth could see that his eyes were fixed straight ahead. The moment Mr. Russo finished the lecture, Bruce bolted into the hallway. As Elizabeth watched him go, she had a sinking feeling in the pit of her stomach. She had a pretty strong hunch that Bruce wasn't going to take Jessica's insult lying down. But she also had to admit that part of her thought Jessica deserved whatever might be coming her way!

Amy shook some salt on her french fries. "It was priceless," she told Lila, who was sitting across from her in the Dairi Burger. "Bruce actually charged into cheerleading practice, his face as purple as that sweater you're wearing. You should have heard him! 'Wakefield, I want a word with you!' And of course Jessica acted completely innocent. She said, 'Do you want to ask me out on another date?' I'll tell you, Lila, I don't think I've ever laughed so hard."

"Then what did Bruce do?"

"Oh, he stomped off, making some vague threat. You know, 'I'll get you for this,' 'You'll be sorry'—that sort of thing."

Lila sipped her chocolate milkshake thoughtfully. It must have been some sight. She knew that Bruce saw himself as an aristocrat, and that no matter how much of a jerk he might really be, he usually succeeded in keeping his cool. "I'm surprised Bruce didn't have more pride than to threaten Jessica in public."

"I'm not," Amy answered. "Even Bruce Patman can be pushed too far. He showed his true colors, that's all." Amy, who had once dated Bruce, was no fan of his now.

"Well, it's not as if Jessica didn't deserve it," Lila retorted sharply. She hadn't forgotten her own grudge against Jessica for having beaten her out of the TV spot—and for reminding her of it at least twenty times a day!

Amy shrugged. "Freedom of the press. And between you and me, Lila, Jessica is right. Bruce *does* sort of kiss like a dead jellyfish."

Amy went on chatting, but Lila didn't hear anything her friend was saying. Her mind was working busily on the seed of a plan. Both she and Bruce had good reason to be mad at Jessica; maybe they should join forces in getting their revenge.

Lila glanced around the Dairi Burger, a popular hangout for Sweet Valley High students. The Dairi Burger was the first place people checked when they were looking for someone. But Bruce wasn't there that afternoon. Probably at tennis practice, Lila guessed. Not that she imagined he'd be in any hurry to stop by the Dairi Burger for some time to come—at least, not until the dead jellyfish jokes died down.

*Bruce.* Lila grimaced. She didn't really want to ask for his help. On the other hand, she *did* want to teach Jessica a lesson. If she could only find a way to trick her ex-friend out of the guest spot on Eric Parker's show so that she, Lila Fowler, could take her rightful place as the star. But a scheme like that would take some doing. Two people would have a much better chance at success than just one.

"Amy, I have to run. Get a ride home with somebody else, OK?"

"But, Li—"

Lila didn't stop to listen to Amy's protests. Grabbing her jacket and purse, she strode purposefully out of the Dairi Burger.

Ten minutes later, Lila pulled into the parking lot adjacent to the Sweet Valley High tennis courts. Perfect timing, she noted with satisfaction. Practice was just over for the day. The members of the boys' tennis team were slipping their rackets into racket covers and toweling the sweat off their faces and necks. From a distance Lila saw one of the guys turn to Bruce, make some kind of remark, and give him a playful slap on the shoulder. Lila could hear the other boys laugh. Obviously the jellyfish jokes were still going strong.

Good, Lila thought. Bruce will still be plenty mad—just the way she wanted him.

"Bruce, over here!" Lila called. "I want to talk to you."

Bruce looked relieved to be called away from his kidding teammates, even if it was Lila who had done the beckoning. Slinging a towel around his neck, he crossed the lawn to where Lila was leaning against the hood of her lime-green Triumph.

"What's up?" he asked, his eyes wary.

*He thinks I'm going to kid him, too!* Lila realized, amused. "I heard that you had a problem with Jess earlier today," she began.

"Look, Lila, if you're going to stick up for her—"

"But I'm not," she assured him quickly. "*Au contraire.* Sticking up for Jessica is the farthest thing from my mind."

"Then what do you—" A knowing gleam came into Bruce's eyes. "Aha. I think I have an idea why you're here."

Lila lowered her thick eyelashes and smiled coyly. "I think that you and I share something, Bruce. A pure and simple desire for revenge."

"What did you have in mind?" Bruce asked, folding his arms across his chest.

"Jessica took something that rightfully belongs to me. The guest spot on Eric Parker's TV program. I want it back, and I plan to get it."

A malicious smile creased Bruce's tanned face. "You know, Lila, ruining Jessica's chance to be on TV also occurred to me as a suitable punishment. But how are we going to do it?"

"Well, I've got a plan. Eric's show is going to be broadcast live from the auditorium at seven-thirty Friday night," Lila said. "Jessica's supposed to be there half an hour earlier, at seven. We just have to make sure that she's nowhere near the high school on Friday night. Then her alternate—*moi*—will take her rightful place in the spotlight. Tell me if you think this would work. . . ."

Lila bent forward and related the particulars of her plan to Bruce. When she had finished, Bruce's eyes were glinting with excitement.

"It's perfect," he said. "It'll take careful timing and a little bit of luck, but I think we can pull it off. I always knew you had an evil streak, Lila, but this time you've really outdone yourself."

Lila beamed. "Thank you, Bruce." She put out her hand and he gave it a firm shake. *He doesn't shake hands like a jellyfish!* she thought. "I think we're going to make a great team."

# Eight

"Help me out here, would you, Jessica?" Elizabeth begged at five-thirty on Tuesday evening. She tossed her sister a cookbook. "I need to find something to make for dinner tonight. Anything, as long as it doesn't take too long to throw together!"

"Why so frazzled?" asked Jessica, dropping onto a stool at the kitchen counter.

"I just got back from taking twenty third-graders on a nature walk around Secca Lake, and I have a ton of homework plus a column to write," explained Elizabeth. She rubbed her forehead. It made her tense just to talk about how much she had to do. "Why don't you cook dinner for once?"

Since both of their parents worked, the twins were supposed to take turns fixing dinner a few nights a week. It didn't always work out quite evenly, however. Jessica had a talent for making excuses, and given Jessica's reputation as a mediocre cook, no one in the family pressed her on this particular chore.

"Look, I'm busy, too," protested Jessica. "I only have three days to prepare for Eric's TV show on Friday!" She flipped distractedly through the cookbook in front of her and tapped her finger on a page. "Here's a perfect recipe: pasta with sun-dried tomatoes. It says it only takes fifteen minutes to prepare the sauce, and Mom brought home a bag of sun-dried tomatoes yesterday."

"Fine." Elizabeth grabbed the cookbook from Jessica and quickly scanned the recipe. "This'll do."

"Well, it's too bad you're so cranky, Liz," Jessica said, "when I'm in such a great mood!"

Elizabeth made a face that seemed to be half scowl, half smile. "Sorry if I'm being such a moper," she said sarcastically.

Jessica didn't even seem to notice her sister's unusual tone of voice. "That's all right. I'm used to you being a moper."

"Gee, thanks!"

"Face it, Liz," Jessica teased. "I'm the life of

93

the party, and you're—well, not a moper but the voice of reason and common sense. That's just the way it is."

Elizabeth and Jessica often joked about being so different in temperament and personality. But Elizabeth did not feel like being reminded of the contrast just now. Still, that was no reason to be mad at Jessica.

Elizabeth sighed with mock-resignation as she put a pot of water on the stove to boil. "OK, I accept my fate. And I'm happy that you're happy. I really am, Jess."

"I know." Jessica took it for granted that her twin shared in all of her victories and all of her defeats. "I still can't believe I'm going to be on national TV, Liz! You know, there's some glory in it for you, too. You're going to be the twin sister of the next big Hollywood star."

"Just what I've always aspired to be!" Elizabeth laughed as she placed several sun-dried tomatoes in a bowl of water to soften.

"It's just too bad that not everyone can be unselfishly happy for me," Jessica observed, her sunny mood suddenly darkening.

"Are you talking about Lila?"

Jessica nodded.

"Well, you can't exactly blame her, Jess," Elizabeth pointed out. "You've been rubbing it in pretty badly."

"Only because she's such a sore loser. It's so much fun to torture her!"

"Nice friend!"

Jessica defended herself. "Anyway, Lila started it by trying to make me miss my interview with Eric."

"You don't know that for sure," Elizabeth reminded her sister.

"I know all I need to know," Jessica insisted. "A little needling is no more than she deserves. Besides, she knows it's just in fun."

Elizabeth recalled what she had seen of Lila at school over the past two days. Lila certainly did not *look* as if she thought it was fun being runner-up or that it was fun being tortured by her supposed best friend. In the end, though, Lila was Jessica's problem, not hers. "Whatever you say, Jess."

Jessica popped up from her seat and started pacing the kitchen. "You know, Liz, I'm psyched to do the show with Eric, but I'm also starting to get a little nervous. The more I think about actually being on TV, on a program that people all over the country watch, the more I think about how easy it would be to blow it. I mean, it's a live broadcast! What if I make a total fool of myself?"

"Obviously Eric has confidence that you'll do just fine on the air," Elizabeth reminded Jessica. "That's why he picked you. You breezed through the preliminary interview last week, didn't you?"

"And the practice discussion today," Jessica conceded. "But that was just the two of us. No one was watching. There weren't any cameras! What if I panic during the real thing?"

Elizabeth laughed. "*You*, panic? Just because a couple of cameras are pointed your way? The sister I know and love is at her best when she's in the spotlight."

Jessica grinned. "I *do* like to be the center of attention. OK, so maybe I won't stutter and blush or trip over my own feet or anything like that. But I could still goof up. What if during the real show Eric asks me harder questions? What if I can't think of anything to say?"

Elizabeth groaned. "What if, what if, what if! Jessica, really!" Elizabeth was running out of patience. She had her own problems right now that Jessica, as usual, didn't know or care about.

"Well—" Jessica put her hands on her hips. "What *if*?"

Elizabeth closed her eyes and counted to ten. "Jessica, you'll be a complete success. Aren't you always?"

Ten seconds had not been long enough to blunt the edge in Elizabeth's voice. Jessica stared at her twin. "No, I'm not always a success," she said matter-of-factly. "I said I was well-rounded—I never said I was perfect. You should know better than anyone, Liz, that there are plenty of times when I need help."

Elizabeth was ashamed. She had never before been anything but one hundred percent loyal to her sister. Lately, though, she had been allowing her own doubts and worries to get in the way of showing her happiness for Jessica. "Then I'll tell you what. If it would make you feel any better, we could put on a pretend talk show. I'll be Eric Parker and ask you some questions. The more you practice talking about the kind of things he's going to ask you, the easier the words will come at the actual broadcast on Friday."

"Would you really do that?" asked Jessica, her eyes shining with gratitude.

Elizabeth was glad she had made the suggestion. "As soon as I finish the pasta sauce," she promised.

Five minutes later, the girls were seated across from each other at the kitchen table. Elizabeth pretended to adjust a microphone attached to her collar. Jessica giggled.

"Welcome to 'Growing Up in America,' " Elizabeth began. "Today we're coming to you live from the auditorium of Sweet Valley High

97

in beautiful Sweet Valley, California. My very special guest this evening is a sixteen-year-old junior at Sweet Valley High, Miss Jessica—"

*Brrng.* "The phone," Jessica observed unnecessarily, making no move to answer it.

"I'll get it." Elizabeth crossed to the wall and lifted the receiver. "Hello?"

"Is this Liz?"

"Yes, it is."

"Liz, it's Don."

"Hi, Don! What's up?"

"A small problem," he answered. "The junior ranger who was scheduled to lead the sunset tour tonight just called to cancel. Can you substitute?"

Elizabeth bit her lip. Dinner, homework, her column, Jessica. But when Don had asked her to be chief of the junior rangers, he had let her know that she would have additional responsibilities. And Elizabeth had willingly accepted the position. She could not let him down now. "You bet, Don. I'll be right over."

"Thanks, Liz. I knew I could count on you."

Elizabeth hung up the phone. "Bad news, Jess. I have to go back to the park for extra duty."

Jessica didn't hide her disappointment. "Oh. Well, maybe we could try this again later."

"Maybe." Elizabeth was already on her way

to the door. "And take over the pasta, would you? See you later!"

"Hi, Mom. Hi, Dad." Elizabeth greeted her parents with a tired smile.

Ned and Alice Wakefield were in the kitchen having a cup of tea. "We were just starting to worry about you," Mr. Wakefield said as he rose to give his daughter a hug. "Jessica said you had to rush back to the lake for some reason. You'd just left when your mother called home. She had wanted to tell you not to start cooking so that we could all go out for a surprise celebration dinner in honor of Jessica's landing the TV spot."

"I'm sorry I missed you. I led the sunset tour from seven till nine," said Elizabeth. She had come straight home afterward, but it was already nine-thirty. She slipped off her bright orange ranger jacket. "It's been a long day. Now I know how you two feel when you work late at the office!"

"Did you get something to eat?" her mother asked. "Why don't I fix you a sandwich?"

"That's OK. I grabbed a burger at the snack bar," Elizabeth replied. "I think I'm just going to crawl upstairs, take a hot shower, and go to bed."

Once in her bedroom, Elizabeth didn't know if she even had the strength to undress. Still in her khaki uniform, she flopped on the bed and closed her eyes.

School, double duty at the park—and it wasn't over yet, Elizabeth realized. She still had homework to do, and her "Eyes and Ears" column for *The Oracle* was only half-written.

Almost ten o'clock. It wasn't really so late; ordinarily at that hour, Elizabeth would simply settle in at her desk and attack her work. But that night she was physically drained from having led two tours around Secca Lake. If she tried to study now, she was sure she would just doze off over her books.

*Why am I doing this, anyway?* she wondered sleepily. It was great to be well-rounded, but in reality she did not feel so much well-rounded these days as split in half. *Am I a writer or a ranger? Can I do both and do them well? Am I going to have to make a choice?*

*I'll think about it tomorrow.* Yawning, Elizabeth rolled over and fumbled with her clock radio. She reset the alarm so she could get up extra early to finish her homework and her column before breakfast.

Elizabeth sat up and started to unbutton the top of her ranger uniform. She noticed the muffled sound of rock music that could always be heard from behind Jessica's closed door suddenly grow stronger. A moment later, the door to Elizabeth's bedroom flew open and her twin sister bounced in.

"You're finally home!" Jessica exclaimed. "Liz, you missed a great dinner with Mom and Dad at Chez Sam! You and I didn't have to make dinner after all. So let's do the interview. I've been thinking up clever things to say all night."

"I can't, Jess," Elizabeth moaned. "I'm totally beat. Can't it wait?"

"Oh." Jessica's bright smile faded. "Well, sure. Whenever you can squeeze me in to your hectic schedule," she added sarcastically.

Elizabeth felt bad. She did say she would help Jessica prepare for her TV appearance. She had come through for Don; now she had to come through for her own sister.

"Hold on. Maybe I'm not so pooped after all." Elizabeth made an attempt to sound animated. "Let's rehearse for *The Eric Parker Show*!"

"Great!" Jessica sat cross-legged on the bed. "I'm ready."

Elizabeth rubbed her eyes for a moment while she tried to think of an opening question. "You asked for it, Jess. Remember, you're dealing with an ace interviewer."

Jessica grinned. "I can take it."

"So, Jessica." Elizabeth adopted a friendly

but serious talk-show-host manner. "Tell me about growing up in Sweet Valley, California. In what ways do you think your experience has been similar to or different from that of other American teenagers?"

Jessica tipped her head to one side, her blond hair falling in a silky curtain. "I think my life is a little of both—similar to and different from other kids," she answered. "I mean, I'm really lucky to live in Sweet Valley. I go to a great school, and I have a wonderful family. I have a lot of material advantages, which unfortunately isn't true for every kid in the United States. But growing up—I think all people my age worry about the same stuff and get excited about the same stuff."

"What do you worry about?" prompted Elizabeth.

"Oh, you know." Jessica laughed. "It really varies. Whether the cute guy on the soccer team likes me and whether or not I'll pass my math midterm. Then there's pollution and world peace and a million other things to think about."

"But you don't spend all of your time worrying?"

"No way!" Jessica declared. "Life is too much fun. The fact that there are a million things to think about is what makes it that way. I like knowing that at any time I can go in a different direction, meet different people, try different things. That's probably the best part of growing up in America."

"Hey, you know what?" Elizabeth asked, momentarily dropping her talk-show-host persona. "You're really good at this!"

"You know what?" Jessica replied. "So are you!"

*This feels right*, Elizabeth thought happily. She and Jessica were not clashing or competing; they were complementing each other. They made a perfect team.

Elizabeth interviewed Jessica for another twenty minutes, asking more challenging questions as well as some silly ones. Jessica handled them all brilliantly. *I am good at this*, Elizabeth decided when they were finished. And she realized something she had forgotten lately: *Not only am I good at this, but I like it.*

Lately writing for the newspaper had seemed more and more as a chore. Nothing she wrote pleased her; the joy she had always found in her journalistic work was missing. But this interview had brought it all back with a rush— how much fun it was to find the story in a person or behind an event.

"Congratulations," Elizabeth said now to Jesica. "You just wowed television viewers all across the nation."

Jessica stretched her arms over her head. "You made it easy, Liz. I wasn't even nervous!"

"Well, I *am* your sister," Elizabeth pointed out. "And we are sitting in my bedroom. It'll be a little different in the auditorium on Friday with Eric."

"But I feel like I have a lot more confidence now," said Jessica. "This really helped. Thanks a lot, Liz."

"Any time, Jess."

The door shut behind Jessica. Elizabeth sank back against the pillows on her bed. Then she sat up straight again. All of a sudden, she was not so tired anymore. In fact, she was in the mood to sit down at her typewriter and rattle off a few more paragraphs of "Eyes and Ears."

Elizabeth jumped to her feet and plugged in her typewriter. Interviewing Jessica, writing up a story—she *did* get a very special satisfaction from this sort of work. But she also loved leading the nature walks at the park.

*I don't have to choose between the two*, Elizabeth told herself as she rolled a crisp sheet of paper into the typewriter. *At least not yet.*

# Nine

"Don't tell me you're going back out in this weather!" Jessica looked at Elizabeth with surprise.

It was Thursday afternoon, and it had been raining hard all day. The world outside the comfortable Wakefield home was wet and gray and not at all inviting.

Reluctantly, Elizabeth slipped her arms into her rain slicker. "I just came home because I forgot to bring my ranger stuff to school. I'm on duty at the park," she reminded her twin.

"I bet people are lining up for nature walks today!" Jessica kidded.

"I'm not scheduled to lead a tour this afternoon," said Elizabeth. That was a bright spot, at least. "I'm running a nature education work-shop for six- to eight-year-olds at the Lodge."

"Better you than me," Jessica said with satisfaction as she curled up on the couch and spread an afghan over her knees. She pointed the remote control at the TV. "So long, Liz. Have a ball!"

"Gee, thanks."

As Elizabeth tramped toward the front door, Jessica flipped to a talk show. It couldn't hurt to get in the mood for her interview. In just a little more than twenty-four hours, she would be on TV herself!

Jessica smiled in anticipation. *No doubt about it, growing up in America is pretty fantastic when a sixteen-year-old can end up on TV just talking about what it's like!*

The phone rang, disturbing Jessica's reverie. She got up and raced down the hallway to the kitchen to answer it. "Hello?"

"Jessica, it's Lila."

Jessica could not believe it. This was a surprise. The two had not spoken civilly to each other in days—not since the announcement that Jessica would be Eric Parker's special guest and Lila the alternate. Jessica had continued to gloat outrageously whenever she got an opportunity. It had been pure pleasure, drawing out her moment of glory. After all, Jessica was still firmly convinced that Lila deserved having her nose rubbed in the dirt for the rotten trick she had played on her.

"Hi, Li," Jessica said blandly. "What's up?"

"I'm calling to apologize," Lila said, sounding uncharacteristically subdued.

"Apologize?" Jessica wasn't sure that she had heard Lila correctly.

"Um-hmm. I'm really sorry about the way I've been acting this week," Lila went on. "Not talking to you and all. I'll admit, I was pretty disappointed that I wasn't picked to be on the talk show. But I've given it some thought, and I don't want to let this TV deal get in the way of our friendship."

"You don't?" Jessica asked, stunned.

"I don't," Lila said firmly. "After all, Jess, by tomorrow night the show will be over, but a true friendship can last a lifetime."

Jessica was speechless. She knew how proud Lila was—this call could not have been easy for her to make. All of a sudden, Jessica was flooded with remorse. She had been enjoying Lila's misery and humiliation and doing her best to make it even worse. And now Lila was the one asking for *her* forgiveness!

"You're right," Jessica said, touched. "Friendship is more important than being on TV."

*Almost*, she thought. "I'm sorry, too, Li. I've been kind of nasty myself."

"Let's put it behind us and celebrate your good luck," Lila said brightly. "I want to make it up to you. How about coming shopping with me tomorrow afternoon? After all, you want to look your absolute best for Eric Parker and the cameras!"

Jessica had gone through both her own closet and Elizabeth's several times already, searching for the perfect outfit. She had not found anything that seemed just right for her TV appearance, so Mrs. Wakefield had promised to take Jessica shopping that evening. "To tell you the truth, Lila, my mother and I were going to go shopping for something when she gets home from work."

"Shopping with your mother! C'mon, Jess. How often do you get to be on national TV? Go with *me*, and I'll help you pick out something great," Lila declared.

Lila did have impeccable taste. And her apology made Jessica feel good. Sure, the two of them were like fire and water sometimes, but Lila *was* her best friend. Besides, her mother would understand.

"That's nice of you, Li," Jessica said warmly. "I'd like that a lot."

"Great. It's a date then," confirmed Lila.

"And you have my guarantee, Jess. We'll find something unforgettable!"

"Thanks for driving," Jessica said as she climbed into the passenger seat of the lime-green Triumph the following afternoon. "Liz took the Fiat to the park."

Lila waved a hand. "No problem."

"So where do you think we should look?" Jessica asked. "BiBi's and the Designer Shop at the Valley Mall?"

Lila glanced over at Jessica. "Oh, let's not go to the mall today," she said casually. "They just have the same old stuff we've already tried on a hundred times." Suddenly, Lila appeared struck by an inspiration. "I know—there's a little boutique in Cold Springs that carries the most gorgeous clothes. Everything's straight from Paris and Milan—styles you won't see anywhere else. Let's go there!"

Jessica raised her eyebrows. "But Cold Springs is an hour up the coast!"

"We have plenty of time," Lila pointed out. "It's only three o'clock. We'll be back by five-thirty, no problem—six at the absolute latest. *And* it's a nice day for a drive."

That much was true. After more than twenty-four hours of rain, the sun had finally broken through the clouds. The whole world seemed sparkling and fresh.

Jessica considered. "Well, maybe."

"I insist," Lila said. "You don't want to appear on national TV wearing anything ordinary, do you?"

Jessica certainly did not. She was ready to be convinced. "They really have great stuff?"

"One-of-a-kind creations. Absolute treasures, and the prices aren't even that outrageous," Lila assured her.

"I'm sold," Jessica declared.

"You'll be sorry," Lila said as she headed toward the coast highway. "I mean, you *won't* be sorry," she quickly corrected herself.

But Jessica had not noticed her friend's slip. As she rolled down her window, she thought of how she had kind of missed these outings with Lila. It just would not have been the same, going in quest of the perfect outfit and accessories with her mother.

*And I'm not going to spoil it by talking about Eric Parker's show*, Jessica decided magnanimously. At any rate, she would not bring up the subject any more than she absolutely had to!

"Li, I didn't get a chance to tell you the most hilarious story." Jessica recounted the story of Bruce storming into cheerleading practice earlier that week.

Lila laughed merrily. "So he really let you have it?"

"Yeah. All sorts of dire threats," Jessica said mockingly. "Which of course were just a lot of hot air. He's staying out of my way."

"Hot air," Lila mused. "That's Bruce, all right."

"Hot air and cold lips," Jessica added, giggling.

Lila drove at the maximum legal speed, and the trip up the coast to Cold Springs seemed to take no time at all.

"This is the prettiest little town," Jessica said as they parked in front of some quaint stucco shops. "Is that it, the Lido? I can't believe you've kept it a secret!"

"I was just holding out for the right moment," Lila said. "This is definitely it."

"For once, I actually have my parents' blessing to charge something." Jessica patted her purse happily.

"Great," Lila said as they entered The Lido. "I wouldn't want you to have a problem paying for the dress of your dreams!"

As Jessica followed Lila to a rack of colorful dresses, she noticed the two saleswomen behind the counter exchange a glance.

"They're staring," Jessica said quietly to Lila.

"It's probably just because we're younger

than most of their customers," Lila replied casually. "They don't think we can afford their stuff."

Jessica cast a superior smile in the saleswomen's direction. "Ha! I guess they don't know that they're looking at a rising star."

Lila put a hand over her mouth, stifling a giggle. "I guess not!"

Jessica flipped through the dresses, looking at the exquisite fabrics and styles. But when she glimpsed a price tag, she gulped. "Pretty steep," she whispered to Lila. "I don't know if my parents' blessing goes *that* far."

"It's a steal for stuff of this quality," Lila stated with authority. She moved on to a rack of two-piece outfits and pulled one out. "Jessica, look at this."

The cropped cherry-red top had big gold buttons, a white sailor-style collar, and a matching miniskirt.

Jessica fell in love with the outfit at first sight. "Oh, how cute!"

"It's perfect," Lila said. "Very French. Sharp, but not too dressy. Go ahead, Jess. Try it on!"

Jessica didn't need any further encouragement. Grabbing the outfit from Lila, she turned to bolt into a dressing room.

"Wait, I'll hold your purse," Lila offered.

"Thanks." Jessica shrugged the bag off her shoulder. "I'll be right out!"

Inside the spacious dressing room, Jessica shed her denim miniskirt and tank top in ten seconds flat. She stepped into the skirt and slipped the top on over her head. Then she pirouetted in front of the three-way mirror, enjoying her reflection. She looked chic and saucy and all-American—the TV cameras were going to love her!

"I have it on, Li. Come see!" Jessica called. Turning slightly, she admired herself from the back. "Li, are you there?"

Jessica knew that it was physically impossible for Lila to set foot in a clothing boutique and not make a purchase; she was probably picking out something for herself right now. Sticking her feet back in her shoes, Jessica stepped out of the dressing room, ready to model the outfit for Lila.

But Lila was nowhere to be seen. Puzzled, Jessica took a few more steps, looking all around the tiny store. Then through the front window of the shop, she saw something that made her jaw drop. Lila was getting into her car! As Jessica watched in astonishment, Lila quickly backed the Triumph out of the parking space.

Without thinking, Jessica dashed to the door and out onto the sidewalk, waving her arms. Where on earth was Lila going?

The Triumph sped away, but before Jessica could chase after it, someone grabbed her arm and twisted it sharply. "Oh, no you don't, young lady!" It was one of the saleswomen from the Lido. "Stop right there!"

"Ow!" Jessica yelped. "Let me go!"

"I don't think so." The woman hauled Jessica back inside. "You're not going to get away with shoplifting from *my* store!"

"Shoplifting?" Jessica repeated in disbelief. "I'm not a shoplifter! How dare you?"

The saleswoman glared at her. Still holding tightly to Jessica's arm, she spoke to the other woman working at the store. "Did you call the police?"

The woman nodded. "They're on their way."

*"Police?"* gasped Jessica. "What's going on?"

The first woman pushed Jessica unceremoniously into a chair by the counter. "You're the one who has some questions to answer, young lady. Why don't you explain why you just left my shop wearing clothes you didn't pay for?"

"But—but I wasn't leaving," Jessica stammered, confused. "I was only looking for my friend. She drove away without me!"

This piece of information did not seem to

interest the women one bit. "We don't know anything about your friend," the first said. "What we do know is what we saw with our own eyes. You can make whatever excuses you like to the police, but it's going to be your word against ours."

Her eyes wide with dismay, Jessica stared out the window at the space where Lila's car had been parked just a moment before. *I'm not a shoplifter!* she thought indignantly. How could anybody think that?

Jessica's throat tightened with an angry sob. She did not know whom she wanted to strangle more, the nasty saleswomen or Lila. *I should have known better than to trust that girl! How could she just drive off and leave me here?*

Jessica bit her lip. It was well after four o'clock, she was fifty miles from Sweet Valley without a car, and she was about to be arrested for shoplifting. In her opinion, walking out of a store wearing a stolen outfit was a pretty stupid way to shoplift, but the fact was that she'd been caught red-handed—she *was* actually wearing the merchandise! And to make matters worse, Lila had her purse! Jessica could not even clear her name by paying for the outfit. How was she ever going to explain her situation to the police and get home in time for the TV broadcast?

Just then, the door of the shop swung open, and two uniformed policemen strode into the store. Jessica took one look at their stern faces and burst into tears.

# Ten

Lila relished every moment of the drive back to Sweet Valley. She did not need the radio or the scenery to entertain her—she was able to entertain herself just by imagining Jessica in handcuffs at the Cold Springs police station, Jessica finally talking her way out of the mess, and Jessica hitchhiking home to Sweet Valley just in time to see Lila on TV with Eric Parker!

Lila laughed out loud as she recalled the glimpse she'd gotten of Jessica in the rearview mirror as she pulled away from the boutique. No sooner had Jessica run out onto the sidewalk in the bright red outfit, waving her arms like a windmill, than a saleswoman had bolted out as well. Yes, Lila concluded, Bruce had played his part as well as she had played hers. He must have been completely convincing when he called the Lido earlier that afternoon, pretending to be a police detective warning the Cold Springs retailers to be on the lookout for a shoplifter answering Jessica's description. The women behind the counter at the shop had been ready to jump on Jessica the minute she stepped into the store.

Lila smiled at her reflection in the rearview mirror. *I really got Jessica this time,* she thought. *Boy, did I get her!* And Jessica deserved it. Lila was sure that Jessica must have used devious means to ingratiate herself with Eric Parker at the preliminary interview. And then the way Jessica had gloated and carried on all week long as if she'd been crowned queen of Sweet Valley High and Lila was only her lady in waiting! Things were much more natural this way, no doubt about it. A Fowler didn't belong anywhere but at the top. Second place was good enough for the likes of Jessica Wakefield.

Lila turned off the highway at the Sweet Valley exit. After driving for a mile on hilly Valley Crest Drive, she braked at the Patmans' driveway. It was after five—Bruce should be home from tennis team practice by now.

She parked the Triumph and hurried along the flagstone path to the back of the hilltop mansion. Sure enough, Bruce had just stepped out of the Olympic-size swimming pool and was in the process of toweling himself off.

His eyes lit up expectantly when he saw her. In spite of herself, Lila took a moment to admire the way the drops of water glistened on Bruce's broad, suntanned chest and shoulders. Then she gave him the thumbs-up sign. "Mission accomplished. Jessica's stranded—maybe even behind bars!"

Bruce punched a fist at the sky. "Yes!" He grabbed Lila and swung her around in a spontaneous victory whirl. "Way to go, Fowler!"

"Way to go, Patman!"

"You mean Detective Tapnam of the Cold Springs police," Bruce corrected her.

Lila giggled wickedly. "It wouldn't have worked without that phone call, Detective. You should've *seen* the way those saleswomen eyeballed Jessica! They were just waiting to pounce."

"Wish I could've been there," Bruce said with regret. "It sounds like we really pulled it off in style."

"It was pretty good teamwork," admitted Lila.

A malicious smile creased Bruce's handsome face. "And so after all her campaigning to win the guest spot on *The Eric Parker Show*, Jessica's not going to be on TV after all. Poor girl."

"It is a shame," Lila agreed in mock sympathy. "Lucky for Eric, he has a gorgeous and fascinating alternate ready to step in and take Jessica's place!"

Her expression grew rapt as she pictured the evening ahead: Lila Fowler on TV with the incredibly handsome, incredibly famous Eric Parker. She was going to be Sweet Valley's woman of the hour. She already had the money and the name—now with the exposure, she'd take off like a shooting star!

Lila threw her arms around Bruce's neck in an impetuous hug. "Thanks for helping to make this happen, Bruce."

Bruce slipped his own arms around Lila's waist. "Any time!"

Suddenly, Lila realized that their bodies were pressed close together. Without thinking, she closed her eyes and tipped her face to his. An instant later, Bruce's lips met hers in a passionate kiss.

They clung together for a moment before jumping apart in confusion. Bruce looked as surprised as Lila did. Lila felt her cheeks burning. Of all people, Bruce Patman! She had never even been attracted to him, and now she had just kissed him. How could she have done it? She didn't even *like* him. Nobody did!

Lila took a giant step backward, just in case

Bruce should get the idea that there was more where that kiss had come from. But Bruce had also stepped back, only narrowly avoiding a plunge into the swimming pool.

Hiding her embarrassment as best she could, Lila acted as if kissing her accomplice were simply a necessary part of the scheme. "Well, I really have to run," she said, her manner blasé. "Time to get ready for the show, you know."

Bruce was just as cool as he gave her a careless wave. "See you at the auditorium."

Lila turned and headed back to her car. All at once, she was very eager to leave the Patman mansion and its resident behind. It was time to get ready. And there was a brand-new dress laid out on her bed at home. She smiled. She'd bought it at the Valley Mall yesterday, and *she* had remembered to pay for it before she left the store!


"That's really the way it happened," Jessica pleaded earnestly. "I was going to pay for the dress—I would never just walk out of a store like that! My parents raised me to be honest. But my friend was driving off without me, and she had my purse."

Jessica gave up with a sigh. It did sound

121

pretty farfetched. No wonder the two officers were raising their eyebrows.

After the police had arrived at the shop, the saleswomen had hustled Jessica back into the dressing room. Jessica had put on her own clothes again, and the horrible red outfit was returned to the rack. Then Officers Brown and Markowitz, Jessica, and Mrs. Loring, the store manager, had proceeded to the Cold Springs police department. Jessica had been forced to ride in the back seat of the squad car, and it had been the most mortifying experience of her life. She did not know which awful feeling was the worst—the fear of not making it back to Sweet Valley in time for the broadcast, the dread of being locked up in jail for the rest of her life, or her fury at Lila, the instigator of the whole mess.

"Did you see another girl?" Sergeant Brown asked Mrs. Loring.

She considered. "There was another girl, yes, and they seemed to be together, but I didn't notice the other girl leave. I was keeping an eye on this one. And I don't believe her story for one minute!"

Sergeant Brown looked at Jessica, and she gazed up at him helplessly. She didn't have to put on an act—she had a feeling she looked as pathetic as she felt. "Well, as it stands we don't have sufficient evidence that Ms. Wakefield actually intended to steal the dress," he began.

"But what about the other shoplifting incidents in the area today!" exclaimed Mrs. Loring. "Detective Tapnam distinctly said—"

"Detective Tapnam?"

"Detective Tapnam," Mrs. Loring confirmed. "He called the shop to warn us that this little thief was making the rounds of downtown Cold Springs. Who knows how many hundreds of dollars of merchandise she made off with before we caught her!"

"But Lila and I came straight here!" Jessica cried. "We didn't set foot in any of the other stores in town."

Sergeant Brown waved a hand. "Let me get this straight. Mrs. Loring, you claim to have received a telephone call from a Detective Tapnam. There is no Detective Tapnam on the Cold Springs force."

"No Detective Tapnam?" Mrs. Loring asked in surprise. "But he gave a perfect description of the shoplifting suspect."

"That's strange, too," interjected Sergeant Markowitz. "There haven't been any other reports of shoplifting today. In fact, we haven't had a shoplifting problem in downtown Cold Springs in weeks."

Jessica looked in confusion from the officers

to Mrs. Loring. A phone call from a nonexistent detective? And then, all at once, Jessica saw the truth. It was all a setup! Lila had planned for Jessica to get nabbed for shoplifting. She hadn't left anything to chance—she had had somebody make a prank call so that the Lido's manager would be primed and suspicious.

*She planned the whole thing*, Jessica realized. *She planned it all so I would miss* The Eric Parker Show! *When I get my hands on that girl, she'll be sorry*. Jessica clenched her fists. Lila might succeed in stealing the TV spot from her, but it would be absolutely the *last* thing she ever did!

"See, I wasn't trying to shoplift the dress," she insisted, appealing to Sergeant Brown, who seemed to be the most sympathetic to her predicament—and the cuter of the two policemen. "I think it was a friend of mine playing a trick on me. I didn't do anything wrong. And please, I really have to go home now. I live in Sweet Valley, and it's an hour away, and if I'm not back by seven o'clock, I'll miss the one chance I'm going to have in my whole life to be on national TV!" Jessica did not have to fake the tears of self-pity that sprang to her eyes.

The two officers turned to Mrs. Loring, who stared sternly at Jessica. Jessica sniffled. "You're saying that the phone call was a prank?" Mrs.

Loring said. "Then I won't press charges. But I don't want to see you in my store again, young lady!"

"Don't worry, you won't!" Jessica promised. She would not be caught dead in Cold Springs after this nightmare shopping trip!

"You're free to go," Sergeant Brown told Jessica. "Thanks for being so cooperative about answering our questions. I'm sorry for the inconvenience."

Jessica jumped to her feet, ready to spring for the door. For a split second she had forgotten she was stranded. How was she going to get home? "What . . . what time is it?" Jessica asked, afraid to hear the answer.

"Twenty-five past six," Sergeant Markowitz informed her.

Jessica sank back into her chair. It was already too late to make it back to Sweet Valley in time for the show, even if she did have transportation—which she didn't, thanks to Lila the traitor.

Jessica felt her eyes fill again. Sergeant Brown patted her shoulder. "I'd be happy to give you a lift down the coast as soon as I get off work at seven," he offered kindly. "Would that help?"

Feeling miserable, Jessica shook her head. "Thanks anyway." She did not care anymore how she got home or whether she ever went home at all. Her dream of appearing on Eric Parker's talk show had been shattered. Jessica squeezed her eyes shut against a flood of angry tears. In just an hour, fans of *The Eric Parker Show* across the country would tune in to see Lila Fowler, not Jessica Wakefield.

"Here." Sergeant Brown handed Jessica a few coins. "There's a pay phone in the hall. Why don't you call your family?"

*Why not?* Jessica thought. She shuffled into the hall, her head hanging.

"Hello?" Elizabeth answered.

"Hi, Liz. It's me."

"Jessica!" Elizabeth cried. "What on earth has happened to you? We're all frantic! Eric Parker wanted you at school at seven o'clock. Did you go right there from your shopping trip with Lila?"

"No, I'm still in Cold Springs. Oh, Liz!" Jessica wailed. "You'll never believe what Lila did to me!" Between sobs, Jessica spilled out the story. "She tricked me out of the TV spot. There's no way I can get home on time—I don't have wings. What am I going to do?"

"Oh, Jess, this is just awful," Elizabeth cried. "I wouldn't have thought that even Lila would stoop so low!" Elizabeth was silent for a moment. Then she exclaimed, "I've got it! Don't worry, I'll take care of everything. Just get to the school as soon as you can."

"I can't," whined Jessica. "I can't bear to see Lila up on stage with Eric Parker!"

"I swear to you that Lila won't take your place on Eric's show," Elizabeth said. "Believe me, Jess. Just get there!"

"But what—?"

Elizabeth had already hung up. Jessica replaced the receiver and shook her head. She would go ahead and take the ride from Sergeant Brown, but she had no idea why Elizabeth would want her to show up at the school auditorium. What did her twin have up her sleeve?

Elizabeth was ready to spring into action. As soon as she hung up on Jessica, she started to bolt into the bathroom. Then the phone rang again. Elizabeth raced back to her night table and grabbed the receiver.

It was Don. "Is this Liz?"

"Yes, it is." Elizabeth knew she'd sounded abrupt. "What's up, Don?"

"Well, it looks like there's an emergency in the making out here at the lake," he explained. "The heavy rains have raised the water level, and some of the nests of the endangered birds along the shore are threatened. We're trying to muster up a team to move the nests. Can you come out and lend a hand?''

Elizabeth gulped. So far, she had never said no to Don's special requests, even when it had meant giving up or postponing some other responsibility. But tonight, she just couldn't be there for him. Tonight, Jessica was Elizabeth's priority.

''Don, I'm afraid I can't. I made a promise to my sister. . . . I really wish I could help, though. I'm sorry—''

''Hey, Liz, it's OK,'' Don assured her. ''I'll call a few of the other kids. You just came to mind first.''

''Are you sure?''

''Definitely. See you at your shift on Sunday.''

'' 'Bye. Good luck.''

Elizabeth knew that Don wanted to make her a senior ranger, and she had been enjoying the time she was spending at Secca Lake. But she was starting to realize that she just couldn't give her all to the park—her heart was some-where else.

# Eleven

"How am I ever going to find something to wear in this mess?" Elizabeth wondered.

As usual, Jessica's bedroom looked like a bargain basement on sales day. Jessica had some very nice clothes; the problem was that most of them lay crumpled on the floor.

*There has to be one decent outfit that's not wrinkled*, Elizabeth prayed, rummaging through her sister's cluttered closet. She pulled a short black skirt from a hanger, grabbed a white tank top from the pile on Jessica's bed, and pulled a boxy turquoise jacket off the back of a chair.

In a few minutes, Elizabeth was dressed in her twin's clothes. She scrunched up the sleeves of the loose jacket, removed her watch, and put on a silver-and-turquoise bracelet and pair of matching earrings. Then she dashed into the bathroom, brushed on some mascara, and dabbed on a bit of lip gloss. Finally, she removed her ponytail holder and shook out her hair.

Elizabeth looked into the bathroom mirror, and Jessica looked back at her. The transformation was complete! She was ready for Eric Parker—and for Lila.

It was already seven o'clock, and there was no time to lose. Elizabeth hurried downstairs and into the kitchen, where her parents and Steven, home from college for the broadcast of the show, were waiting anxiously.

Mrs. Wakefield glanced at her daughter, turned to her husband, and then back at Elizabeth. "Jessica, when did you get home?" she asked in surprise.

"It's about time!" said Steven. "Where's Liz?"

"We'd better leave for the auditorium this minute," Mr. Wakefield declared.

Elizabeth stifled a giggle. It was tempting to let her family go on thinking that she was Jessica; it would be a good warm-up for trying to fool Eric Parker, and the entire Sweet Valley High student body, and everyone who would be watching the show at home! But it was probably better to reveal the truth to her family—Elizabeth needed their support.

"It's me—Elizabeth. I'll explain in the car. Just get me to the school, fast!"

It was nearly seven-fifteen when the Wakefields arrived at Sweet Valley High. Elizabeth sprang out of the car before Mr. Wakefield even had time to come to a complete stop. "I'll look for you after the broadcast!" she promised.

"Good lucky, honey," her parents called after her.

"Go for it!" urged Steven.

Anticipating a crowd at the front entrance of the school, Elizabeth had had her father drop her off at a side door. Now she hurried inside and started down the hall in the direction of the main lobby. As she approached, she could see the long line of students waiting to be seated in the auditorium. She could not go in that way, that much was for sure; she could not risk blowing her cover. Elizabeth retreated back down the hall and ducked through a door marked "Backstage."

Members of Eric's camera crew were rushing about. Elizabeth hid behind an old prop so that no one would spot her just yet. Then she saw the people she was looking for: Eric Parker and Lila.

Eric, a puzzled frown on his face, was checking his watch. Lila, holding a dress bag, stood at his side, smiling sweetly.

"I'm afraid it looks as if Jessica's not going to make it," Elizabeth heard Eric say. "I can't imagine why she hasn't gotten in touch with me. If something came up—"

"I can't imagine," Lila echoed innocently.

Eric grew businesslike. "Well, Lila, you'd better get ready to take her place. We're on the air in a few minutes!"

"I'll change and be right out." Lila waltzed off in the direction of the girls' dressing room, smiling triumphantly.

*Lila looks like the cat that swallowed the canary,* Elizabeth thought with disgust. *Well, it's time to give her a taste of her own medicine!*

Elizabeth darted out from her hiding place. As soon as Lila had closed the door to the dressing room behind her, Elizabeth stuck a chair, probably an old prop, underneath the door handle, wedging it tightly. That should do the trick. Lila was not going onstage now; in fact, she was not going anywhere!

Elizabeth hurried back to Eric, who was reading over some notes.

When he saw Elizabeth, his eyebrows shot up. "Jessica, you're here after all!" he exclaimed. "I'd given up on you."

"I wouldn't have missed this for the world,"

Elizabeth assured him. "I'm sorry if I gave you a scare. My twin sister could tell you, I'm never on time for anything!"

He laughed. "That's right—you were late for the interview last week. Well, are you ready?"

Suddenly, Elizabeth was hit with the enormity of what she was about to do. She was about to be interviewed live on national TV! And she was about to be Jessica Wakefield! Elizabeth could feel the butterflies take flight in her stomach.

"I'm ready," Elizabeth answered with her best imitation of Jessica's bubbling manner.

"Great. Then let's go!"

Eric put a hand on Elizabeth's back and ushered her onto the stage. As they took their seats, members of the crew fussed around them, adjusting light meters and microphones. Through the lowered curtain, Elizabeth could hear the excited buzzing of the audience.

Minutes later, the curtain went up and the cameras started rolling.

"Welcome to Sweet Valley, California, my hometown," Eric Parker began. "Tonight I have a very special guest who's going to share her perspective on growing up in America. Ladies and gentlemen, meet Jessica Wakefield!"

\* \* \*

"Thank for the ride," Jessica said to Sergeant Brown as he braked his squad car in front of the main entrance to the high school.

During the one-hour drive to Sweet Valley, Jessica had shared the whole story of the battle for the TV spot and Lila's last, cruelest deception—or at least as much of it as she'd been able to piece together.

"No problem, Jessica." Sergeant Brown smiled sympathetically. "I'm sorry you didn't get to be on TV."

"Maybe next time," she answered glumly. But Jessica seriously doubted there would be a next time.

"Stay out of trouble, OK?"

Jessica waved goodbye, then turned and trudged into the main lobby. She paused before the double doors that led into the auditorium. It was almost eight o'clock—the half-hour interview was probably just concluding. Jessica didn't really want to go inside and witness Lila's moment of stolen glory. It would be far too painful. Still, Elizabeth had pressed her to hurry straight to the high school. There must have been a reason for Elizabeth's urgency.

Jessica pushed the door open a crack and slipped quietly inside. From her vantage point at the rear of the dark theater, she gazed forward at the two people seated onstage. She steeled herself to see that snake Lila, all charm and smiles, in the midst of bamboozling the whole United States into thinking that she was the sweetest, most all-American thing ever.

Then Jessica gasped. *That's not Lila*, she thought in astonishment. *That's me!* No—of course it was not her. It was Elizabeth!

Her head spinning, Jessica listened to her twin carry on a witty discussion with Eric Parker. She had to admit, Elizabeth was dóing a pretty good Jessica impersonation. And the audience seemed to love her performance. Jessica could hear pockets of clapping and laughter.

"Your life sounds like a whirlwind, Jessica," Eric Parker was saying. "How do you find time to do all the things that interest you?"

Elizabeth tipped her head thoughtfully to one side. "I guess . . . priorities," she said. "It's not always easy to figure out what matters most to you or what you do best, but once you do figure it out, then you just have to put your energy there."

Jessica frowned. What was Elizabeth talking about? Priorities? Jessica didn't even know the meaning of the word! The kids in the audience were sure to recognize Elizabeth's masquerade if she got serious all of a sudden!

"What would you say are your top three priorities, Jessica?" Eric continued.

Elizabeth smiled mischievously, the dimple in her left cheek deepening. "Boys." There was laughter from the audience. "Suntanning. And I guess—boys again."

Jessica breathed a sigh of relief. That was more like it!

"Seriously," Elizabeth continued. "I can't pretend—having fun is what I like to do best right now. But the way I see it, anybody who doesn't make the most of being young will regret it when they're grown up and working nine to five and dealing with *real* responsibilities."

*My opinion exactly!* Jessica thought. Suddenly it occurred to her that she had better get out of the auditorium before the interview ended and the lights came back up. She could not risk her schoolmates seeing her and wondering why there were two Jessicas in the same room.

Back in the corridor, Jessica paced up and down, unsure of what to do next. Then she thought of the backstage door. *Why not?* she decided. There was no one around to stop her.

Jessica passed through the door and immediately spotted Lila. Hands on her hips, her face dark with rage, Lila was watching Elizabeth's interview. Clearly, she was seething at having been outwitted.

Jessica stuck her tongue out at the back of Lila's buttercup-yellow dress. *Serves you right!*

Just then, the interview came to an end. As Elizabeth and Eric rose to their feet and shook hands, the audience cheered wildly. Lila pivoted. In order not to be seen, Jessica sprang through the nearest door and into the girls' dressing room.

Eric and Elizabeth stepped backstage. For a few moments, they stood chatting, Elizabeth facing the dressing room and Eric, who had his back to the door.

Jessica caught Elizabeth's eye over Eric's shoulder. Elizabeth excused herself to Eric and joined her twin in the dressing room. As soon as the door was safely locked, the twins threw their arms around each other.

"Liz, you were fantastic!" Jessica shrieked. She was so grateful to Elizabeth for coming to her rescue and turning the tables on Lila that she was not even jealous that *Elizabeth* had been the one who had been interviewed and not herself. "I want to hear absolutely everything. What did Lila do when she saw you? What other questions did Eric ask you? What was it like being on TV? Start at the very beginning!"

Elizabeth put a finger over her lips. "We can talk about it later," she whispered. "Just get out of those clothes, quick!"

Jessica stared at her twin for a second, then grinned. She hugged Elizabeth again. "Liz, you are the best, most loyal and generous and all-around wonderful sister in the whole world!"

Elizabeth knew that Jessica meant every word she said, and it made her very happy. Of all the times she had come to her twin's rescue, Elizabeth had a feeling that this escapade would remain in her memory as particularly meaningful. It was kind of ironic, but standing in for Jessica tonight had helped Elizabeth to see something about herself. She had not lost anything these past few weeks by helping Jessica to be the best person she could possibly be. Jessica's triumphs did not take anything away from Elizabeth.

"Shut up and strip!" Elizabeth ordered with a smile.

A minute later, the twins had swapped outfits, right down to their earrings. When Jessica emerged from the dressing room in the black skirt and turquoise jacket that Elizabeth had been wearing during the interview, she was immediately mobbed by friends who had rushed backstage to congratulate her.

A short while ago, she had been completely dejected; now, thanks to Elizabeth, Jessica was enjoying the stardom that was rightfully hers. She basked in the shower of compliments.

"You were great!" Amy gushed.

"It was a breeze," Jessica said with a shrug.

"What an interview!" Cara squeezed Jessica's arm. "You'll be hosting your own TV show next!"

Winston high-fived her. "Way to go, Wakefield!"

"Come back and visit someday when you're rich and famous," Ken Matthews teased.

Jessica laughed. "Don't worry, guys—I'll never forget my humble roots! After all, Eric Parker didn't, right?"

More friends crowded around, and Jessica had a smile for everyone. She was enjoying the attention immensely—as much as if she had actually earned it herself!

But Jessica kept her eyes peeled. Would Lila have the nerve to face her after the stunt she had pulled that afternoon in Cold Springs?

Yes, it seemed she would. Lila had reappeared, her face twisted with fury. But she was not scowling at Jessica. Instead, her stormy eyes were trained on Bruce Patman, who was lurking on the edge of the crowd.

*Why would Lila be mad at Bruce?* Jessica wondered.

She watched curiously as Lila plowed her way over to Bruce. When they were face to face, Lila opened her mouth and yelled, "Thanks a lot for screwing things up, Patman! Obviously your stupid phone call wasn't very convincing if the police couldn't keep Jessica occupied any longer!"

So Bruce had been in on Lila's plan—he was the one who had made the phone call! *I get it now*, Jessica thought. *Patman, Tapnam. Duh. Good old Bruce!* After "The Worst Dates of My Life" episode, Jessica supposed she should not be surprised.

Bruce was speechless, but Lila still had something on her mind. And by now the entire crowd of students had been captivated by Lila's rage. "And Jessica was right all along. You *do* kiss like a dead jellyfish!"

Jessica couldn't imagine how Lila would possibly know that for sure, but she joined her friends in their loud laughter. His face purple, Bruce Patman turned on his heel and marched away, his dignity in tatters.

Lila began to flounce off in the other direction, her car keys in her hand.

"Not so fast, Lila!" Jessica called as she hurried after her. When she was close enough, Jessica snatched the keys from Lila's hand. "Let me see those."

"Hey—what!" Lila shrieked as Jessica tossed the keys high up into the air, where they got snagged in a rolled-up curtain. "Why'd you do that? How am I supposed to get home?"

Jessica recalled Lila zooming off in her Triumph and her own ride in Sergeant Brown's police car. She had absolutely no pity. "That's your problem!"

# Twelve

"I love the fact that my mom and dad are proud parents. You know, they were in the audience the night of Eric Parker's special broadcast," Elizabeth told her friends the following Monday as they ate their lunch. "Unfortunately, they went one step too far."

"What do you mean?" asked Neil Freemount.

"They also taped the interview on the VCR." Elizabeth smiled. "So guess who sat in front of the television all weekend watching herself over and over?"

Neil, Penny, and Enid laughed. Elizabeth caught her boyfriend's eye, and he winked. Todd was the only one besides her family who knew that Elizabeth had filled in for Jessica at

142

the last minute. She had to share the secret with someone.

Elizabeth was not kidding about Jessica having watched the videotape over and over again. Jessica had played it so many times that she had learned all of Eric's questions and all of Elizabeth's replies by heart. Elizabeth suspected that Jessica had managed to convince herself that it was actually she, not Elizabeth, on the tape after all.

Elizabeth took advantage of the rest of her lunch period to revise an article for *The Oracle*. She reread a paragraph, then made a few changes with a red pencil.

Todd put an arm around her shoulders. "Happy?" he whispered in her ear.

"Yes, I am. Although it was hard telling Don yesterday that I couldn't be chief of the junior rangers anymore."

"From everything Enid said, you were his star recruit."

"I'll miss volunteering at Secca Lake," Elizabeth told him. "I realized, though, that if you take the idea of being well-rounded too far, you just end up being overextended. I was trying to do too many things at once."

Todd held her eyes for a moment, and Elizabeth knew that he understood. Most important, Elizabeth had discovered that she had been wrong to doubt her writing and reporting talents. Sure, she had run into some obstacles—lack of inspiration, the threat of Jessica's literary achievement—but she would never have been happy abandoning her writing out of jealousy. As she had learned during her interview with Eric Parker, Jessica's achievements didn't detract from her own.

"Working at the park—I knew I was part of a great cause," Elizabeth continued. "But it's not the kind of work you can do halfway. It takes commitment."

"So does being a writer," said Todd.

"Exactly." Elizabeth smiled at him. "And writing's what I love most. I'm sure of that now."

"You can make a difference in the world by writing, too," Penny reminded her.

"That's what this article is all about." Elizabeth tapped the top sheet with her pencil. "It kind of brings it all together for me. I'm writing about the program at Secca Lake and the importance of environmental awareness. I'm hoping it will inspire more students to participate in local conservation programs. One final good deed for the park, you know?"

"I'll put it on the front page," Penny promised. "And that reminds me." Penny pulled a typewritten page out of her notebook. "Would you add this to the bottom of next week's 'Eyes and Ears'?"

"What is it?" asked Elizabeth.

"Just a list of new faces at Sweet Valley High," Penny explained. "There's a new guidance counselor and two teachers moving up from the middle school, plus a few new students. One's a junior," she added. "Have any of you guys met Andrea Slade?"

Elizabeth and the others shook their heads.

"If she's worth knowing, she'll find her way to us sooner or later," Todd joked.

Elizabeth gave him a playful shove. "Conceited!"

"Hi, everyone!" Jessica breezed up to the table, lunch tray in hand, Amy and Cara following in her wake. "Is there room for us?"

"Of course!" Elizabeth pulled out a chair for her twin.

"Still flying high?" Todd asked Jessica.

Elizabeth kicked him under the table. "Don't encourage her!" she whispered.

"Oh, I'm getting used to being the school celebrity," Jessica replied airily. "My hand's kind of cramped from giving so many autographs, though!"

Elizabeth shook her head and went back to reading her article, a smile on her face.

Jessica unwrapped her sandwich, cheerfully

humming the latest Jamie Peters single. She was on top of the world. She had decided that when you got right down to it, it did not matter that it had been Elizabeth who was interviewed by Eric Parker on national television. The fact was that everybody *thought* it was Jessica—so it might as well have been! She was the one who was getting all the attention: her name was the one in the local newspaper, and she was the one the talent scouts would be calling any day now.

"There she is," Cara whispered to Amy.

Jessica was just about to take a bite of her sandwich when Amy grabbed her left arm and Cara her right. The sandwich went flying. "What's going on?" Jessica yelped. "Look at my sandwich—all the sprouts fell out!"

"I'll buy you another one," Cara promised. "C'mon! Before you eat, you have to talk."

Cara and Amy hauled their friend out of her seat and propelled her toward the back of the cafeteria. "Talk about what?" asked Jessica. "Oh, I suppose somebody else wants to hear all about what it's like to be a TV star."

Amy giggled. "No, that's one story you're not going to need to tell *this* person."

"Here we are," announced Cara.

Lila sat all alone at a corner table eating a chef salad. She and Jessica eyed each other warily.

"Entertaining all your friends, I see!" Jessica jeered.

"Excuse me, these seats are taken," Lila said coldly. "No space for liars and cheats and manipulators."

"Because the biggest liar, cheat, and manipulator in the entire world is already in residence!" Jessica retorted.

"Whoa! Stop right there," Amy commanded. "Cease fire."

"This is a peace mission," Cara explained. "We don't want to hear any backtalk—you don't have a choice. Make up or else!"

"Or else what?" Jessica asked.

"Or else Amy and I are going to start a feud of our own," Cara threatened, only half teasing. "Against you two!"

"I didn't keep exact count of how many times you guys stabbed each other in the back," Amy said. "But it seems to me that the score's pretty much even."

"Lila started it," Jessica swore. "She almost made me miss my tryout interview with Eric Parker. And then she ditched me in Cold Springs so I'd miss the real thing!"

"You didn't, though," Cara pointed out, "and that's what really matters."

"All's well that ends well," Amy agreed cheerfully.

"But it didn't end well," Lila complained. "How on earth did you manage to get back to Sweet Valley in time to make it onto the show?"

Jessica crossed her arms, smiling smugly. "It's my little secret."

"So we're all friends again. Right?" Cara urged.

"Why not?" agreed Jessica. After all, she had nothing to lose. She'd come out the winner!

"I suppose," Lila grumbled.

"Well, how about we seal the deal with a shopping trip after school?" Amy suggested.

Jessica and Lila looked at each other in horror and burst out laughing. "I *guess* I'll be safe." Jessica grinned. "With Amy and Cara along to protect me, that is. And this time, we take *my* car!"

"Well, are you guys going to sit down or not?" asked Lila, still pretending to be huffy but smiling in spite of herself.

"First, somebody owes me another sandwich! Turkey with avocado and sprouts," Jessica instructed Cara. "Oh, Li. See that girl over there? She's wearing the exact same skirt I've been dying to buy at Lisette's!"

The girl in the brown suede miniskirt was standing in front of one of the vending machines. Lila and Jessica watched as gorgeous but arro-

148

gant Kirk Anderson approached her. He made some kind of invitation; the girl shook her head with a smile. Then she turned her back to him and punched a button on the machine.

"Kirk the Jerk struck out," Amy observed.

"I'm surprised," Lila said. "She's new. She wouldn't know about Kirk's reputation yet."

"What's her name?" asked Jessica.

"Andrea Slade. I have a class with her. She's actually kind of a nerd, sort of mysterious and shy."

"Well, I like her taste in clothes anyway," Jessica remarked. "She looks funky."

"She looks like a loser to me," Lila countered as the new girl left the cafeteria. "No one really interesting ever moves to this town!"

*Is there anything interesting about the mysterious Andrea Slade? Find out in Sweet Valley High #72,* ROCK STAR'S GIRL.

149

| | | | |
|---|---|---|---|
| ☐ | 27567-4 | DOUBLE LOVE #1 | $2.95 |
| ☐ | 27578-X | SECRETS #2 | $2.99 |
| ☐ | 27669-7 | PLAYING WITH FIRE #3 | $2.99 |
| ☐ | 27493-7 | POWER PLAY #4 | $2.99 |
| ☐ | 27568-2 | ALL NIGHT LONG #5 | $2.99 |
| ☐ | 27741-3 | DANGEROUS LOVE #6 | $2.99 |
| ☐ | 27672-7 | DEAR SISTER #7 | $2.99 |
| ☐ | 27569-0 | HEARTBREAKER #8 | $2.99 |
| ☐ | 27878-9 | RACING HEARTS #9 | $2.99 |
| ☐ | 27668-9 | WRONG KIND OF GIRL #10 | $2.95 |
| ☐ | 27941-6 | TOO GOOD TO BE TRUE #11 | $2.99 |
| ☐ | 27755-3 | WHEN LOVE DIES #12 | $2.95 |
| ☐ | 27877-0 | KIDNAPPED #13 | $2.99 |
| ☐ | 27939-4 | DECEPTIONS #14 | $2.95 |
| ☐ | 27940-5 | PROMISES #15 | $3.25 |
| ☐ | 27431-7 | RAGS TO RICHES #16 | $2.95 |
| ☐ | 27931-9 | LOVE LETTERS #17 | $2.95 |
| ☐ | 27444-9 | HEAD OVER HEELS #18 | $2.95 |
| ☐ | 27589-5 | SHOWDOWN #19 | $2.95 |
| ☐ | 27454-6 | CRASH LANDING! #20 | $2.99 |
| ☐ | 27566-6 | RUNAWAY #21 | $2.99 |
| ☐ | 27952-1 | TOO MUCH IN LOVE #22 | $2.99 |
| ☐ | 27951-3 | SAY GOODBYE #23 | $2.99 |
| ☐ | 27492-9 | MEMORIES #24 | $2.99 |
| ☐ | 27944-0 | NOWHERE TO RUN #25 | $2.99 |
| ☐ | 27670-0 | HOSTAGE #26 | $2.95 |
| ☐ | 27885-1 | LOVESTRUCK #27 | $2.99 |
| ☐ | 28087-2 | ALONE IN THE CROWD #28 | $2.99 |

Buy them at your local bookstore or use this page to order.

---

Bantam Books, Dept. SVH, 2451 South Wolf Road, Des Plaines, IL 60018

Please send me the items I have checked above. I am enclosing $_____
(please add $2.50 to cover postage and handling). Send check or money
order, no cash or C.O.D.s please.

Mr/Ms _____

Address _____

City/State _____ Zip _____

SVH—3/92

Please allow four to six weeks for delivery.
Prices and availability subject to change without notice.